This Made Me Think of You

Mark Brennan Rosenberg

ISBN-13:
978-1530601974

ISBN-10:
1530601975

for George

September 17, 2014 at 11:14 AM

Facebook:

Gretchen Edwards is now single.

From: Max Roberts
To: Gretchen Edwards
This Made Me Think of You
September 17, 2014 at 6:46 PM

Gretchen –

This afternoon, I found myself walking through Times Square. Don't ask me why. I had a job interview (the one I told you about the other day) and began walking up Broadway from Madison Square until I found myself on 42nd Street, in the middle of the alleged crossroads of America (if the "crossroads of America" are filled with McDonald's and Disney Stores, we're all doomed.) I couldn't help but think of you. Looking at all of the glimmering lights and tourists scurrying to Madame Tussauds, I remembered that time we had tickets to whatever the hottest show on Broadway was five years ago that you were dragging me to and it was raining and there were tourists everywhere just as there were today. Of course it was pouring when we got out of the subway in Times Square and we were without umbrellas. There were swarms of people, all of whom seemed to be bumping into each other, not knowing where to go. Frazzled -- your blond hair that you had meticulously styled for the evening now dripping wet -- you literally picked up an elderly Asian woman asking for directions and moved her out of your way. My God, we laughed so hard about that. It may have actually been funnier than the damn show we saw that night. You never had time for tourists and it always made me laugh. As I walked up Broadway this afternoon, that thought crossed my mind. You've been on my mind all day.

I can't believe it's over between us. When you're in a relationship -- or in a relationship for as long as we have been in one -- you never think it's going to end. I honestly don't know what to say. Things ended so badly between the two of us, so much was said that wasn't meant, so many things happened that can't be taken back. Ten years is a long time and I don't want to give up on you. I know you're mad at me, but things can change. I can change. I can go back to being the man that you fell in love with ten years ago.

Instead of harping on the past and pointing fingers, I have decided to send you a note every day for as long as I can and share a memory of something that made me think of you. You don't have to reply -- or even read them, but I want you to know how much I am still thinking about you. I know it's only been a day since you ended things, but it's hard to walk down the streets of New York and not think of something that leads my memory straight back to you.

I will love you forever and I promise you, if you decide you'd like to work on our relationship, I can make things better between the two of us.

Forever,
Max

From: Max Roberts
To: Gretchen Edwards
This Made Me Think of You
September 18, 2014 at 9:16 PM

Gretchen –

I hope that you got my email from yesterday. I know I said you didn't need to respond, but I hope you at least took a glance at it. I thought you'd at least get a chuckle from that Asian tourist memory, because it always used to make us laugh so hard, but I suppose the cheese stands alone on that one.

I don't know if you saw this on Facebook but I read that Liz Archibald's mother died last night in her sleep. She was kind of a bitch to you in college (especially when she started that nasty rumor about you and I having that threesome) so I don't even know if you follow her on Facebook anymore, but she seemed really bent out of shape about it, as I image she would be. This made me think of you. Remember a few years ago when my mother passed away? When we went back home to Baltimore for that week that never seemed to end? You were such a huge support system for my family and I. In fact, I'm not sure what we would have done without you there. Remember when we came back to my mom's house after going to the cemetery and you sat in her old rocking chair, sipped on a beer and smoked an imaginary cigarette just as she used to and critiqued what everyone was wearing?

"You wore that to my funeral?" you barked at my sister, taking a swig of Miller Lite. We all howled with laughter through our tears. You always had a simple way to make things that seemed impossible to get over somehow manageable. It's a rare gift that very few people have. I don't know what I would have done if you hadn't been there for us. In fact, stupid things happen to me almost every day that I get bent out of shape about and I just imagine you standing by me saying: "Max, is this problem really that extraordinary that you won't be able to move on with your day?" Granted, they weren't nearly as bad as losing my mother, but you have a comforting way about you that always set my mind at ease. I wish you could set my mind at ease over our breakup.

I saw a girl that looked like you on the subway today. She was tall and skinny. A blond, with black-rimmed glasses that were just like yours, reading a book. My heart stopped for a moment, in the hopes that it was you. I thought to myself: *What am I going to say to her? Should I beg on my hands and knees for her to come back to me? No! The subway floor is too dirty for that and I also have some pride left. I think.* When she looked up at me, she smiled. Then her smile quickly turned to a frown when she realized I had been staring at her like a madman, running through possible scenarios of what I would say if it happened to be you in my head. I was so embarrassed. Every time I turn a corner I think I see you, but you're never there.

I hope that we can speak soon. I know that after the breakup you said you needed space and that I hurt you, but I would really love it if we could communicate, if for nothing else than to catch up and see how you are doing. It's very weird seeing someone for ten years straight then not speaking to them at all. It feels as if someone has died, but I know that you are somewhere – here in New York – still living your life, you just happen to be doing it without me. It's odd.

Forever,
Max

From: Max Roberts
To: Gretchen Edwards
This Made Me Think of You
September 19, 2014 at 3:36 PM

Gretchen –

I haven't heard a peep from you in three days. No status updates, no pictures on Instagram, no texts, nothing. This is the first time in ten years that we've gone without talking for more than a day. It's the hardest thing I have ever had to do. It's harder than giving up drinking. This has been such a difficult time for the both of us. Losing you, having to sublet an apartment with people who are basically strangers to me, not having a job and running out of money has been a lot for me to understand and to cope with. I know you said you would always be there for me no matter what and I think I need your help now. Coming back to New York after moving to California and then trying to cope with this breakup has been a lot for me to deal with mentally and financially and I'm unsure of who I can turn to, because since our breakup it's still not clear who's still my friend and who's just yours now.

I know I told you I would write you once a day and tell you something that made me think of you and today it was simply everything -- I don't know how to put it any more eloquently. I thought men were supposed to deal with these things better than women were. I go back and forth between what happened in the past and where we are now and it doesn't seem to make much sense. I keep racking my brain to try and come up with a reason that would explain this whole situation away but I can't. All of my casual acquaintances say the typical bro things to say: "move on" and "you'll find someone else" to which I reply: "fuck you, I will move on when I am good and ready" and "have you met Gretchen? There is no one else after her." I know there are other fish in the sea, but you're my fish. How are you handling this breakup? Since we aren't speaking, my mind is racing, thinking of how you could potentially be feeling and what exactly it is that you are doing. I've thought of so many different scenarios that race through my mind each day. Does she have a new beau? Is she happier without me? Is she miserable? It's like trying to do a book report without ever reading the book – I'm making up what I think is happening to you without any concrete evidence and it's driving me a bit insane.

I know our relationship was rife with problems and I am really beginning to understand my place in all of that. When we moved to New York from Baltimore after college, we were bright eyed and hopeful and our future was seemingly filled with endless love and happiness. We loved living in New York. I don't know why I made us move to California. You always said that I was going to become some big, famous television writer and would leave you for a younger, prettier woman. Isn't it coincidental that we moved to California, came back to New York and you're the one who ended up leaving me? I let it all get in the way of us and I'm sorry, I shouldn't have. I let the unattainable usurp what was sitting right in front of me.

I didn't get that job that I applied for the other day, just in case you were wondering. I knew I hadn't when I left the interview, but I held out hope because you always told me that I needed to if I ever wanted to get a job that paid well instead of just writing books and jumping from low-paying part-time job to low-paying part-time job. And you are right. When I went into the interview, I knew just by the air of the room that I hadn't gotten it. I just had a feeling, I can't explain it. I walked into this big conference room with a long, sleek, expensive looking table in the center of it and two bored looking, privileged twenty-something douche bags sat at the end of it. The girl must have been hungover because I swear to God she was seconds away from falling asleep at the table and it was noon. The guy acted as if my writing and publishing two books was something that happened every single day in New York. Maybe it does. Neither of them were very impressed with my résumé or accomplishments. They were more consumed by how fast I could churn out click bait and what "attention grabbing" headlines I could come up with. I don't know if I'm cut out to write for things like that. I know it's really the only thing I'm qualified to do (besides write books – which we both know doesn't pay as well as everyone assumes it does) but it frightens me to think that my future could just amount to me sitting in an open air office grinding away on my laptop producing garage articles like "Bisexuals Have Voices Too", "Meet the Baby Panda Who's Poop Looks Like Jesus", and "How You're

Being Racist, Even After You've Adopted a Black Child." I keep trying because I told you I would never give up and I won't. I remember when we got back to New York after I failed to make my mark in California a few weeks ago and I threw my hands in the air and said: "Gretchen, I give up! I can't do this anymore." And you told me: "Max Roberts does not give up and that's not what I signed up for." So, I'm trying. I'm trying because you never stopped believing in my career no matter what obstacles were hurled in my direction.

I wanted to tell the two twenty-somethings on the other end of the table, so self-righteous with their lattes and fake watches, that they weren't special and the only thing that made them any different than their parents and the generation before them was that they grew up with an iPhone in their hand, but I refrained from doing so. I guess it really wouldn't have mattered, since I didn't get the job anyway.

I hope work is going well with you. Any news about that big promotion?

Forever,
Max

From: Max Roberts
To: Gretchen Edwards
This Made Me Think of You
September 20, 2014 at 12:31 PM

Gretchen --

You know how sometimes old people who are in relationships for decades die one after the other and people always say the person who died second "died of a broken heart"? I wonder if that could happen if the other person is still alive. Sometimes, I think about you and the things we used to do and it takes my breath away. I stop dead in my tracks and have to remember to breathe. It's the oddest sensation. I used to feel this way occasionally after my mother passed, but this is different. Can you even die of a broken heart?

Remember when we were in college and I was drinking too much during finals? The last year we were in school -- remember that? When we went to the Inner Harbor in Baltimore and I was so wasted that I fell and hit my head on that weird 1980's looking fountain thing that's so out of place that sits in the middle of it? You took me to the hospital and I swore up and down that I would never drink again. The next day when I woke up, my ego as sore as my head, I stepped foot into my first AA meeting with you by my side and took a twenty-four hour chip. It was the most humbling experience of my life. But you were always there for me. I'm almost eight years sober now and I don't think I would be without you. Today, I went to my first AA meeting in years and it made me think of you. How proud you were of me for every accomplishment, how you helped me count my days and even remembered milestones when I had forgotten them. AA is such a weird place but it always makes me think of you. I love how it is such a hodgepodge of different people who are all there for the same reason but who you feel are all secretly judging you for no reason – from bums on the street to upscale socialites – it's such a mixed bag but no one ever seems to question it. I went to a meeting in a midtown church this morning. The topic was regret, which was certainly apropos. There was an older gay man there and he told this story about how for years he had been friends with this guy who lived in his neighborhood, and one day his friend turned around and told him that he was in love with him. The man who was telling the story said that he didn't know what to do or say to his friend, because he didn't feel that he loved him in return. He stressed over it for years and finally, one Christmas morning, he realized that he had been wrong all along and called his friend to tell him that he truly was in love with him too but that he was simply too scared to tell him earlier. But when he called on that Christmas morning he found out that his friend had died the morning before. He's never loved anyone since and that was thirty years ago. Can you imagine? It broke my heart. I hope that you decide you want to try and make things work but also that you don't find me dead on a Christmas Eve morning, with the cat having eaten off part of my face. That would be devastating.

Forever,
Max

Facebook:

Sept. 21, 2014 at 11:43 AM

Gretchen Edwards: Off to my happy place for a weekend with my girlfriends!

Tweet:

Sept. 21, 2014: @maxrobertsauthor: "this longing may shorten my life."

From: Max Roberts
To: Gretchen Edwards
This Made Me Think of You
September 21, 2014 at 7:09 PM

Gretchen –

I saw on Facebook that you were "off to your happy place for the weekend" and if I know you, you were having a girls weekend in Atlantic City. That was always our special place. God, we are like eighty years olds. We sure do love trash (and coupons, buffets, staring into the ocean for seemingly endless amounts of time and penny slots, lol). And we love things that used to be nice and glamourous. I don't know what the word for that is. I am sure I could Google it, but I don't want to lose my train of thought.

My sister was in town this weekend. We had a laugh when she got here because I told her that of course the weekend that my girlfriend broke up with me is the weekend that literally every single one of my Facebook friends decided that they were going to get engaged. Every single mother fucking person was basking in their happiness, while I'm over here sitting in front of my computer, crying into a pint of Ben and Jerry's, alone. Not that I really cared, it just seemed like a miserable coincidence. Like when the release of Adele's last album coincided with my mother's death. A cruel joke from God, I tell you! Natalie tried to lift my spirits this weekend and I suppose it was nice to have her around. Considering I'm now subletting an apartment with strangers, it was nice to have someone that I knew around (besides Robert, as cats can't talk or give you much more than a cuddle. I talk to him, but he never really says anything in return). It's so weird living in New York with the cat and without you.

Natalie and I were just sitting around on Sunday morning and it was kind of nice out so we decided to go to Coney Island. Of course this made me think of you. Going back to that feeling of liking things that used to be glamorous (what is that word?) Coney Island is certainly that. Natalie and I walked along the boardwalk and all I could think of was our first trip there. Two crazy kids from Baltimore with Nathan's hot dogs strolling the boards like it was 1905. Looking around us, we always imagined what it would be like if the island (which isn't even an island anymore) was still filled with the luxurious pleasure palaces of the Golden Age instead of what it was today (read: ghetto fabulous but still amazing). Imagining taking the plunge in the parachute jump back in the 1950s and screaming for dear life! It was always so crazy to me that Coney Island was once considered the premiere resort destination for so many and just like Atlantic City is such a dump today. You and I always managed to see the beauty behind the faded, frenzied colored design.

Natalie and I took a ride on one of the swinging carriages of The Wonder Wheel and I swear to God she screamed even louder than you did the first time we rode it together. She said to me: "I don't trust that something built in 1920 isn't going to kill me in 2014". I told her that the first time we had ridden it, I Googled to make sure there hadn't been any incidents on it and that she would be fine. It is pretty remarkable that the Ferris wheel still holds up today and that no one has ever been killed on it. Ha. I was glad to see my sister, but I must admit, getting through the weekend was hard without you. She lent me some money, because I am a bit cash poor these days after moving across the country and back within the time frame of six months. I know you said that you would help me out through this transition but it's not your responsibility so don't bother worrying about it (if you even were). This coming week, I am working at a school in Brooklyn. They are short a janitor and one of my old friends from high-school, Kyle (I don't know if you ever met him?), knew that I was looking for work and suggested me to the super intendant. So, if you need me, I'll be mopping up vomit somewhere in Rockaway. It's not glamorous, but it will help with bills. I can't seem to find anything permanent right now, so I have to take what I can get. I'm actually happy to do it. Not only because I need the money, but cleaning and doing menial labor has always helped me focus for one reason or another.

I have come to realize that it's not what you do that makes you who you are, which is why I really don't care about being a janitor this week. I know I stressed over it so much when we were in California and I thought I was going to be this big famous writer, but now I realize that I would be happy being a janitor at a crappy school in Brooklyn if it meant that you were by my side.

I hope you had a fun weekend. I really miss you and love you.

Forever,
Max

From: Gretchen Edwards
To: Max Roberts
RE: This Made Me Think of You
September 21, 2014 at 10:01 PM

Max —

The word is neophile. Someone who has a strong affinity for novelty.

Yes, I was in Atlantic City this weekend. I was supposed to go with Claire and Becky but Becky got sick and Claire had a last minute event that she had to attend with Bruce, so I ended up going by myself.

Listen, I really appreciate the emails and I think it's very sweet of you - I really do, but you have got to try and move on. I asked you for some space after this breakup and it seems as though you are completely incapable of giving it to me. I need time to process everything that has gone on between the two of us. California was such a mess and you made me feel like complete shit the entire time we were there. I know that that's not you and I know that things were crazy out there, but it doesn't erase the way you made me feel. You yelled at me, you screamed at me, you called me names, you blamed me for everything that happened to us while we were there, most of which was completely out of my control. I don't deserve to be treated like that. You had done it before we left for California but never as frequently as when we were there. You have got to get a handle on your temper. It's not you. Maybe you can take this time to figure out your own problems.

I transferred my job to our Los Angeles headquarters last year because you were done living in New York and you wanted to explore possible opportunities out there. But once we got there, I was the only one making any money and you couldn't handle the constant rejection, so for whatever reason you took it out on me. We lived in a shitty apartment so far away from everyone else and were miserable because we couldn't make ends meet. We turned into a one income home and I don't know if it was because you were embarrassed that you couldn't take care of me anymore or felt like a failure or what, but it wasn't working. I suggested that we come back to New York after six months because I thought it would help our relationship and finances and the second we got back you acted as if it was my sole responsibility to find us an apartment and get us settled when you knew I didn't have much money either. I gave you everything I had and it never seemed to be enough.

You called me garbage, Max. I know you didn't mean it and I know you've since apologized relentlessly for it, but it hurt. I know you are hurting right now. However, I need to stop being mad at you before we can truly sit down and have a conversation about what happened between the two of us in the past year.

I'm glad you've started going back to AA meetings. Remember how much that helped you? Take this time to take care of yourself.

I did get the promotion. Just to let you know, starting in a few months I will be traveling for work five days a week so I won't really be around much. Maybe my not being around so much will help you move on a bit.

Please stop with the emails. It's upsetting me.

Gretchen

From: Max Roberts
To: Gretchen Edwards
RE: This Made Me Think of You
September 21, 2014 at 11:15 PM

Gretchen –

I'm sorry I have been upsetting you with my emails. I just thought it would be a nice way to let you know that I am thinking of you and that I am sorry for what happened. I thought that if I was able to remind you of the good times that we shared that you may have a change of heart or something. I guess not. I will give you all of the space that you need. There's nothing that doesn't make me think of you and it's hard. I will start going back to AA meetings regularly and have been taking much better care of myself.

How does a week of space sound? Maybe we can catch up next weekend or something? Just let me know. I'm pretty free. Max

Text exchange:

September 22, 2014

Max: I'm sorry for calling and getting so upset on the voicemail I left. (12:03 AM)
Gretchen: It's OK. (12:04 AM)
Max: I didn't mean to anger you. I'm just so saddened by all of this. (12:04 AM)
Gretchen: Max, it's OK. Just give me some space. (12:05 AM)
Max: OK. Love you. (12:06 AM)
Gretchen: Love you too. (READ: 12:06 AM)

From: Max Roberts
To: Gretchen Edwards
RE: This Made Me Think of You
September 29, 2014 at 9:40 AM

Hi Gretchen –

I called you earlier to see if you wanted to get together this weekend, but I never heard back from you. It's OK if you don't. I just wanted to let you know that I have gone to an AA meeting every day this week and I am really starting to feel a lot better about this situation. I'm still heartbroken, but I guess what I am trying to say is that I'm learning how to express my feelings a bit better. I thought I was very angry when you first broke up with me and now I am realizing that I wasn't angry, but my feelings were very hurt. Those are two different emotions and finally, after thirty years on this earth, I am beginning to understand the difference between anger and sadness. A grown man being this sad, have you ever heard of anything...well...sadder? I've been told over and over to "feel my feelings" and to not feel bad about being upset over this situation and I am attempting to do just that. Feeling your feelings actually kind of sucks, because it's just left me upset.

There was a gentleman at the meeting that I went to this afternoon named Brett. He had been sober for about five years and his girlfriend had recently broken up with him too. He kind of reminded me of Don Rickles, only about fifty years younger. He's wise cracking, short, fat and bald, lol. He told the group that he had borderline personality disorder, which I thought at first was multiple personalities, but apparently those are two different things that daytime television never clearly explained the difference between. He lamented that he would go from being very happy to thinking that the world was ending the very next day. These feelings, paired with his alcoholism, hindered his dealing with his issues in a productive way. I began to think that maybe that's what was wrong with me. He said that one little thing would trigger him and set him off into a tirade and he couldn't handle his anger, sadness or even happiness, depending on the trigger. After the meeting, I confronted him and asked if there was anything I could do, because I felt the same way that he did. He said that there was no medication that I could take because there is no medication that helps BPD and that therapy was the answer. I don't have health insurance right now so I asked him if there was anywhere I could go for free and he told me about this place in the village that has complimentary therapy sessions for people who can't afford to pay for it. I think I'm going to do that on top of AA. I pretty much self-diagnosed myself with this (although Brett helped by confirming; mind you, neither one of us are doctors so we may both be full of shit) but free therapy has certainly never hurt anyone. I was told today by another AA that I am grieving a loss, and like a death I need to work through my problems the best way I know how.

I know you don't really want to speak to me right now, but I take comfort in the fact that I can still let you know what I am up to, even if you never read or respond to these emails. Like I said, it's uncomfortable not knowing exactly what you are up to, but I hope you're well. Perhaps we can meet this weekend for a chat?

Forever,
Max

From: Max Roberts
To: Gretchen Edwards
RE: This Made Me Think of You
September 30, 2014 at 1:12 PM

Gretchen –

I'm worried about you. You said you were going to get back to me, but I haven't heard anything from you and I've
checked Instagram and Facebook (to make sure you weren't dead. Promise.) You're nowhere to be found. I hope everything is OK.

You know how I hate the weather changing. I know you hate it too. We always said that everyone loves fall so fucking much but no one ever realizes that it lasts for like a day in New York and it's just a segue into a misery that is winter, after weeks of a nice cold side rain. Today was the first day that felt really chilly, like fall was coming. This made me think of you. You would always moan about the "basic white bitches" as you called them, celebrating the fact that they could now enjoy their cardigan sweaters, Ugg boots and pumpkin spice lattes while you longed for summer. You always loved the summer. You really are more of a summer girl than anything else. You love the beach so much, which is why I find it so ironic that we hated California with such a passion. I wonder what all of those basic white bitches in California are up to. Probably drinking iced pumpkin spice lattes for all I know. I do know that I certainly don't care.

I am really working my AA program and am starting to feel better about myself. I'm also going to group therapy tomorrow with Brett which should be interesting, if nothing else. Do you think there's a possibility that we could meet up this weekend? I have a few things I need to say to you and I think I'd rather do it in person if you don't mind.

I love you Gretchen, Max

From: Max Roberts
To: Gretchen Edwards
RE: This Made Me Think of You
October 01, 2014 at 4:44 PM

Gretchen –

I really wanted to see you this weekend -- which clearly isn't happening since the weekend is gone. It's OK, I know you're busy! I don't think I can hold what I wanted to speak to you about in person off much longer. I wanted to give you a 9th Step amends. I don't know if you know this or not (or remember the first time I did this with you when I first stopped drinking) but the 9th Step of Alcoholics Anonymous is where you apologize for the things that you've done that have hurt other people. When I did it with you the first time, I mainly apologized for my behavior when I was drinking. But this time I really want to apologize for everything that has happened since, of which there has been a lot, so please bear with me. I am releasing this animosity and letting it go. I am not mad about any of these things and I have no more resentments towards you, but I want you to know that I am sorry for the way I acted. In AA, once you make amends, you make a conscious effort to never make the same mistakes from the past again and I will do my very best to hold up my end of the bargain. Anyway, here goes:

I'm sorry for getting angry with you when I got back from my second book tour. None of that was your fault. I was frustrated due to lack of sleep and having to pay for the whole tour myself and not selling a lot of books on the road. It was not your fault. I repeat: it was not your fault. I understand that it was two years ago and you may have probably already forgotten about it, but I haven't and I need you to know that I was just frustrated with how things turned out and I never should have put that back on you. I should have never held onto that resentment and I'm sorry it affected us so poorly.

I'm sorry for holding money over your head when I got back from the book tour. I know that I gave you what I could to help get you through school and paid for us to move to New York but that was eight years ago.

It's water under the bridge and I don't want any of it back. I'm basically a pauper with only a laptop and pair of jeans to my name now. The money doesn't matter to me anymore and I am sorry for bringing it up. Money is fluid, it comes and goes, and I was happy to give it to you when you needed it.

Looping back to my last point, I am sorry for taking my feelings out on you when they weren't your fault. Just, in general.

I'm sorry for blaming you for what happened California. I know it was my idea to move there, but initially I was going to go out for a few months alone and feel it out so that we wouldn't get stuck there and so that I would have a place to come home to in New York if it didn't work out. You wanted to go because you wanted to try something new, to go on this adventure with me and that didn't work out for us but it's not your fault. I know when we were there I blamed you for the situation we were in, but honestly, if you weren't there I don't know what I would have done without you. I'm sorry for the way I treated you during that time. It wasn't fair. You had every right to come with me and try something new and it's not your fault that it didn't work out.

I'm sorry for my dependency upon you in California. That was not the way that I had intended for things to turn out. I thought that when we got there I would have no problem getting a writing gig because the agents who I had spoken to before we got there said that it would be so easy for me to transition into writing for television or film because I had published two books. I see now that that was not the case. I'm sorry for always having to rely on you for everything when we were there. It's not fair and it's not how a boyfriend is supposed to treat his girlfriend.

I'm sorry I barely spoke to you on the five day car ride back to New York. I felt defeated, like a loser. I couldn't make it work in California and I was upset. I shouldn't have taken that out on you. It was not your fault.

I'm sorry for forcing you to single handily try to work things out for us once we got back to New York. It was not your responsibility to take care of finding an apartment for us when we got back here. I know you said you would take care of it once we returned, but to lay all of that on you, it just wasn't right and it led us to where we are today. I'm also sorry for saying that I was giving up once we got back. I was in a dark place when we returned home and that has passed, believe me.

Finally, and most importantly, I'm sorry for the incident that happened once we got back to New York. We were so broke. Neither one of us had eaten in days and I lashed out at you over twenty dollars. It was wrong and unacceptable. I know that we were both doing what we needed to do to get by. You were fortunate enough to have your fancy fashion job with offices in both New York and Los Angeles and could effortlessly transition back to the east coast. I was not so lucky. When we got back and had to live separately in order to save money, it was such a change – we had never lived apart. I was forced to do manual labor to make ends meet because I couldn't find a writing job and was so hungry after three days of not eating that I forced you to give me the only money you had. That's not fair and I shouldn't have done it. I will never forgive myself for it because I know that was the final straw that broke the camel's back. We were in survival mode and my instincts were not to take care of you (which they should have been) but instead on me, me, me. Typical Max.

I felt like such a failure when California didn't work out and I blamed you for it then blamed you once again for me not being able to get back on my feet once we got back to New York. None of this was your fault. I realize now, after really learning to explore my feelings a bit more productively (there's some more AA banter for you) that I was grasping for the unattainable. I was not content with what I had (and we had a lot in New York: I had you, we had a place to live, we had the cat, I had a job that I hated but paid me) and got greedy. I am very lucky to have had two books published. That's what all writers long for. I shouldn't have given up what we had here for something that could have been in California. Before we left, it was as if I had planned this story as to what was going to happen once we got to Los Angeles. We'd move into a cute bungalow in Santa Monica, I'd write for a hit television show, you'd work your way up the corporate ladder and we'd go to parties and be the toast of the town. Everything would be great. Unfortunately, that's not what happened. I think when you project an image of what you want and how you are going to get it, you are always going to be disappointed because it never really works out the way you hope. It's a dream that's never capable of coming true. I should have recognized a good thing when I had it. We really love New York. We were so glad to be back once we returned that I could have gotten down on my hands and knees and kissed the dirty ass sidewalk. I know things were hard but now that we are a bit more settled and you have your place and I have mine, maybe it's time to open a dialogue again and start talking about our feelings. I realize through AA that I haven't been honest with myself about what my feelings actually are. I turned everything into rage and anger, when in reality I was upset and disappointed. It wasn't fair.

On a different topic, I had a bit of a breakdown last night after I emailed you that I wanted to share. I went outside to smoke a cigarette and I bumped into Brenda Graham, remember her? Turns out, she lives in my neighborhood here up in Washington Heights and she reminded me that we left a few things in her storage unit before we left to go to L.A. Remember when we thought we could pack eight years of a New York apartment into a small Jetta? The night before we left we had so much stuff that we hadn't put in our storage unit that we had to call Brenda to tell her that we needed to use her storage room for some of our things and that we would send her money to have them sent to California when we got there but never did because we were never settled? Ha. This made me think of you. You were SO convinced that your Tetris pathos was going to pay off when it came to packing all of our shit into that small ass car. God I miss our furniture. I wish we hadn't sold everything. I wish we hadn't gotten rid of our old apartment. When I retrieved everything from her storage unit and caught up with her a bit, I took our old things to my new home and found a few things that made me think of you. First of all, we had about forty vases in our old apartment. I'm not entirely sure what the fuck we needed so many vases for. Were we robbing funeral homes for old bouquets of flowers at one point in our relationship? And remember that old candle holder that your parents brought back from Mexico that somehow managed to light up the entire room even when you put the smallest candle in it? God it's so ugly. But I had a candle that I bought at the store the other day for ninety-nine cents and I put it in the holder last night and it lit up my entire bedroom. For whatever reason, this prompted me to cry myself to sleep. Having feelings has been the worst.

I'm going to group therapy with Brett (my new AA friend) tomorrow night. I am nervous, but I do think I may have that BPD thing, even though I've pretty much convinced myself I have it with little-to-no evidence to fully support this whatsoever. BPD sounds more like a urinary tract infection than a mental disorder. I will let you know how things go.

I love you Gretchen,
Max

From: Gretchen Edwards
To: Max Roberts
RE: This Made Me Think of You
October 01, 2014 at 11:09 PM

Hi Max –

I'm sorry I'm responding so late. I am alive, thank you for your concern.

I'm actually going through it quite a bit myself right now. As I told you a few weeks back, I have accepted a new position at my company and I will be traveling about five days a week. I am working out the logistics with them and I'm afraid that they're not really offering me enough money to travel with for expenses and I really need to make sure that this is taken care of before December because I don't want to be put in a bad situation while I'm on the road. We both know from experience how troubling that can be.

I hear what you're saying, Max. I very much appreciate your thorough list of apologies. I am really not mad at you. Perhaps, I was a bit out of line when I originally said that I was. I think I just need time and some space in order to get over everything that happened. You are right about what you said about the twenty dollars. It was my last twenty dollars that I had for the week and I gave it to you and you were still so hurtful to me that it made me feel terrible. That's not how a man is supposed to treat his girlfriend and I know that we had really been through it with the California move and your ego was bruised but I was certainly not the person to take it out on. At that point, I had done everything in my power to take care of us and you screamed at the top of your lungs at me over twenty bucks, which I gave you anyway but it still wasn't enough. I gave you everything I had and I know it wasn't much but it still wasn't enough for you. That's not the Max I know. That's not the Max that I fell in love with ten years ago. Maybe that Max doesn't exist anymore? I tried to move past that, but it stayed with me and hurt so bad that finally I just couldn't do it anymore.

I appreciate and accept your apology. I think it's very big of you. I know from listening to my girlfriends who have gone through breakups in the past that admitting you are wrong in a situation is rare and the fact that you can even do that shows a lot of strength on your end. It doesn't, however, change my position on this relationship. We are still broken up and I still need time to process everything that has gone on between the two of us. I know you need to change some things about your life, and I know that I do as well. I need to have more confidence in what I am about to do and rebuild my energy that I may have lost in the move to and from California and in this relationship. Also, you never apologized for that email you sent me directly after our breakup. That hurt, Max.

I'm sorry, but I just can't be with you right now. Let's talk in a little while and see where our heads are at. I still need some time before I can even think about getting back together with you.

Gretchen.

P.S. I looked up BPD. I think you may just be bi-polar. When you get on your feet, you really should see a therapist.

From: Max Roberts
To: Gretchen Edwards
RE: This Made Me Think of You
October 02, 2014 at 9:27 PM

Gretchen –

Thanks for getting back to me. How exciting about your new job. I know how hard you worked for that. I do also know, from experience, that being on the road like that can be taxing and I am sure you want to cover any and all loose ends before your journey begins. I know it won't be until December that you start traveling like that, so maybe we can try to work all of this out before then? I know you're still upset with me and I can only apologize so much. Tell me what you want me to do to make this better and I will. I promise.

I appreciate your remarks that I might be bi-polar, however BPD may be more manageable for me to deal with right now because it doesn't require medication and bi-polar does. Since I'm self-diagnosing and don't have insurance, this might be the way to go. I did, however, go to group therapy with Brett last night. I guess it made me feel better. I definitely related a lot to what everyone was saying. I guess with BPD, much like with alcoholism (a double whammy), you project either the very best or absolute worst possible outcome of every single scenario. This made me think of you because sometimes when you would ask me to go for a run and I would decline in order to stay home and write, I would always feel like you were going to come back from your run and breakup with me. Like my not wanting to exercise was going to somehow make or break our relationship. It's preposterous to think that way and I am certainly going to get a handle on it, I will tell you that much right now.

I'm sorry about the email that I sent immediately following our breakup. It was wrong. Not only did I send a list of reasons why everything was your fault (it wasn't) I also had the nerve to sit and type up a detailed description of money you owed me, which was completely wrong and unacceptable. I was angry and hurt and I acted inappropriately. I'm sorry for that too. I truly am. My helping you through school and helping you get settled when we initially moved to New York eight years ago were things that I did out of love for you and I in no way expect you to pay me back. My first instinct after we broke up was anger because I was caught by surprise. I never thought we'd break up – it never crossed my mind. So when we did, I became very angry, which I think is natural. I shouldn't have, however, taken that anger out on you. I'm very sorry.

I am making ends meet cleaning houses right now and writing once a week for a pretty lame but quite prosperous online magazine that's paying me $150 a week (hey, hey, now we're in the big time!) I wish I knew more about what you were up to. It's such a weird feeling knowing that you are out there living a life I know nothing about.

Maybe we can grab coffee sometime before you start your frequent travels?

I love you Gretchen.
Max

From: Gretchen Edwards
To: Max Roberts
RE: This Made Me Think of You
October 02, 2014 at 11:35 AM

Max —

I really can't be with you right now. That list of what I "owed" you was completely out of line and I am not one hundred percent sure you understand that. Yes, you helped get me through school. I will forever be indebted to you for that. But you must remember that I helped pay for EVERYTHING when we were in California. Don't forget that when you were off taking meetings and schmoozing, I was bringing home the bacon and paying for literally everything while we were there. It's inappropriate to bring that up and was absolutely disgusting that you even suggested that I owe you in the first place.

I think we need to cool it. These trips down memory lane and reminiscing over things past are too much for me to deal with right now. I have a lot on my plate, training for my new position while working my normal hours along with dealing with this breakup. I know you don't understand this, but even though I am the one who broke up with you, I am still very much upset about it. I lost my best friend too. I'm trying to distance myself and focus on work and moving ahead in life and I know you don't have a lot going on right now, which I am sure is stressful and annoying, but you can't harp on the past forever. It's not healthy and you said you wanted to get better.

Please just take a break. Do things that you like to do and be happy.

Gretchen.

From: Max Roberts
To: Gretchen Edwards
RE: This Made Me Think of You
October 03, 2014 at 8:14 AM

Gretchen –

You don't have to be so cold. I understand my place in how things went down and I truly am trying to make them better, I really am. But you have to see things from my point of view. I somehow turned into a monster during our time in California. I feel completely at fault for what happened between us and you don't seem to understand how that feels. I feel like after ten years I am owed a little bit more than just a few email exchanges. You won't pick up the phone when I call and you won't respond to my requests to meet up for coffee. You're so focused on the bad things that have happened between the two of us and all I am trying to do is make you see that there was a lot of good there too. I understand your position, however. I understand that you need to focus on all of the bad things that happened between the two of us because it makes you more comfortable in the decision you made in breaking up with me. I get it. There was a lot of good there too. There is still good stuff there. If there weren't, I wouldn't be trying so damn hard. You wouldn't have wanted to move to California with me if there wasn't, so please try to see things from my point of view. I fucked up. I know it. You're almost acting – in the way you seem to be effortlessly getting over me – that I was a summer camp fling that lasted for a few months. This was ten years, Gretchen, come on.

Yesterday on the subway I was picking my nose and some woman looked at me like I was a carnival side show freak. I forgot that you were the only person in the world who was not only not bothered by that but were immune to my farts, especially when they smelled like rotten vegetables. That's love. The people I am currently living with are not immune to them, I will tell you that right now. The cat hates them too. He says "hi" by the way. Remember him?

Still sorry, Max

From: Gretchen Edwards
To: Max Roberts
RE: This Made Me Think of You
October 03, 2014 at 10:17 AM

Max –

Please. Stop.

Please stop this. I'm not trying to be cold, I am trying to move on. I am not going to get back together with you right now. I hate to say this over email, but I don't want to get into over the phone. There's nothing left. Your behavior was too much for me and I have nothing left to give you right now. Please respect the way I feel. I am emotionally spent from the past year of our lives. It was all too much and I need a break. Please respect that. And yes, I remember the cat. Thank you for taking care of him. Seeing him or you right now would be way too much for me to bear.

Gretchen

Text exchange:

October 03, 2014

Max: Gretchen, if something happens, please know that it is not your fault. (11:16 PM)
Gretchen: What? (11:16 PM)
Max: If I start drinking again or whatever, it's not because of you. I need you to know that. (11:17 PM)
Gretchen: Where are you? (11:17 PM)
Max: Home. (11:18 PM)
Gretchen: Are you going to drink? (11:19 PM)
Max: I don't know. (11:19 PM)
Gretchen: Can you call someone? Have you found a new sponsor? What about that Brent guy? (11:20 PM)
Max: Brett? I spoke to him earlier and I went to two AA meetings today. Not helping. (11:21 PM)
Gretchen: Max, you've worked so hard on this. Don't let our breakup ruin almost eight years of sobriety. (11:21 PM)
Max: I'm sorry (11:21 PM)
Max: I'm sorry (11:21 PM)
Max: I'm sorry (11:21 PM)
Max: I'm sorry (11:21 PM)
Gretchen: MAX ENOUGH! I know you are sorry. I know you love me. I know you want me back. You have told me these things relentlessly for the past two weeks. It's not going to change how I feel about you and the fact that I need time. (11:22 PM)
Max: I'm sorry (11:23 PM)
Gretchen: Please, don't drink. (11:24 PM)
Max: I'm dying without you. (11:24 PM)
Gretchen: Max, you are a level headed person. You are an asshole sometimes, but I know that you know that drinking right now is not going to make anything better. (11:25 PM)
Max: I'm sorry, I shouldn't have reached out. I should have texted or called another AA. (11:26 PM)
Gretchen: Just because we aren't together, doesn't mean that I don't care about you anymore. I am here if you need me. (11:28 PM)

Max: Thanks. (11:28 PM)
Gretchen: Please, don't drink. (11:29 PM)
Max: OK. (11:29 PM)
Max: I love you. (11:30 PM)
Gretchen: You too. (READ: 11:30 PM)

From: Max Roberts
To: Gretchen Edwards
RE: This Made Me Think of You
October 04, 2014 at 10:20 AM

Gretchen --

I am truly sorry about last night. I should not have texted you. Honestly, my alcoholism is not your responsibility or concern and I didn't mean to worry you the way that I did. I didn't drink and I won't drink ever again if I can manage it. Maybe I should just say: I won't drink today, like the program tells me to. But I don't want to get you worried about anything. I am fine.

It's very hard for me to try and give you space. I guess, I am just coming to terms with all of the changes in my life right now and none of them are making a ton of sense. It's really a lot at once. We lived together for so long and now I am subletting this apartment and I have to be honest, it's weird. I think the people I live with think I am a lunatic. I very rarely ever see them and when I do it's usually right after I have come home from cleaning someone's house and I think they're too embarrassed for me to ask me anything about myself. It's also weird because, since I am subletting, none of the furniture here is mine. All I brought with me was a bag of clothes as I haven't had time to get anything out of our storage unit. You're the only one with the key. I feel like a stranger in the home that is supposed to be my own. Not having a full-time job is hard too. Even when I was writing my books, I still had another job to keep me busy. Now, I'm cleaning toilets and running people's errands. It's humiliating. But it's what I have to do to get by now so I just have to do what I have to do.

A few things happened yesterday that triggered my texting you last night. First, I went to a woman's house who had posted an ad on Craigslist. She said that she needed her entire apartment cleaned and was willing to pay a pretty hefty sum for a few hours work, so I accepted the offer. Cleaning is actually kind of cathartic. It gives me a few hours to just be with my thoughts and when I'm done I can actually see that I've accomplished something. I just cleaned a house, hooray! I can see my finished product within hours of beginning it. It's not like writing a book, which takes forever. But what bothered me was that the woman whose house I was cleaning knew who I was. She follows me on Twitter and apparently has read both of my books. I insisted that I wasn't who she thought I was but she kept pressing me until I finally gave in. She was so condescending about the fact that I was cleaning her house. "Why would you have to clean my house if you're some big, successful author?" she asked me. I told her that it wasn't the 1980s and that everyone with a laptop was essentially an author at this point and she just laughed in my face.

Secondly, my father called and asked how you were doing yesterday morning. He is insistent upon the fact that we will get back together. It's heartbreaking to hear him talk about how much he loves you. He told me that he still considered you as a daughter no matter what happened between the two of us and would always be there for you, if you needed anything. Just in case you were wondering.

It's painful to tell you this, but I might as well just get it off my chest. He had given me my mother's engagement ring to give to you when I went down for a quick visit once we got back to the east coast (and before you ask, yes Natalie was pissed that she wasn't getting it, but loves you so she let it slide). I had planned to propose to you on your birthday next year. My plan was to whisk you away for a ghetto fabulous weekend of penny slots and buffets in Atlantic City (how we do) and afterwards take you for a stroll along the Boardwalk and propose. I had it planned down to the last detail. AC is our spot and I knew you would love it. I was planning on waiting until after your birthday because it's far enough away that I supposed that the dust from this whole California debacle would have settled by then and we'd be in a better spot. You had, for such a long time, asked me if I wanted to get married and for the longest time I protested because I figured that since we lived together and we shared a life together, what was a stupid piece of paper going to prove? We were together for ten years, which I know is a long time to be together and not get married, but I'm a pussy sometimes when it comes to full-on commitments. On our way back from California, I thought to myself that if we could make it through everything that we went through there then certainly we had made it through the rain and the future was brighter for us on the other side. I guess I was wrong (for now?). I'm not telling you any of this because I think you are going to run back into my arms if you knew I had a ring and was going to propose. I guess I am telling you this because I really was listening to what you were saying, even though I may not have always shown that.

Again, I am sorry for what happened last night. It won't happen again.

I love you Gretchen.

Max.

From: Gretchen Edwards
To: Max Roberts
RE: This Made Me Think of You
October 05, 2014 at 9:15 AM

Max —

Oh, Max. I don't know really what to say to any of this. I am sorry about your experience while cleaning that woman's house. That must have been horrible.

I don't know what to say about the ring. It's nice to hear, but I don't know what to say.

I've asked you repeatedly for time off and you seem incapable of giving it to me. I'm not in love with you anymore. I love you, but I'm not in love with you and I don't want to be with you right now. I don't know how to say it any clearer.

Please give me some space. I really need to deal with my issues on my own. I have a huge meeting with my boss coming up and I don't feel prepared for it and this isn't helping. Let's cool off and speak in a month or so.

Best,
Gretchen

From Max Roberts
To: Gretchen Edwards
RE: This Made Me Think of You
October 06, 2014 at 12:23 AM

Gretchen --

I will give you space, if that's what you'd like. I promise I will back off. Please just don't forget about me. I will never forget about you.

And I will love you forever,
Max

From: Gretchen Edwards
To: Max Roberts
RE: This Made Me Think of You
October 06, 2014 at 9:12 AM

M —

Never. I could never forget about you.

G

Instagram:

Oct. 18, 2014

MaxRobertsAuthor: A picture of sidewalk art saying: "Love is the answer"

Venmo:

Oct. 21: Gretchen E. to Connie F. "Champagne for Meeting"
Oct. 24: Gretchen E. to Becky C. "Girls night out! Wooh!"
Oct. 27: Gretchen E. to Claire G. (Sassy Girl Emojis)

Tweet:

October 27, 2014:

@maxrobertsauthor: "Just listened to "Can't Let Go" By Mariah Carey twenty times on repeat, lol."

Facebook:

October 28, 2014 at 6:17 AM:

Gretchen Edwards is feeling hungover. "Too many margs last night."

From: Max Roberts
To: Gretchen Edwards
RE: The Made Me Think of You
October 30, 2014 at 10:19 AM

Gretchen --

It's been almost a month. It seems as though you have been very busy and
having a great time (at least from what I can tell via your cavalier
Facebook posts). I was hoping that we may be able to speak soon, if you
were up for it.

I have to tell you something that made me think of you the other day. I
was walking down the street and happened to be listening to
the playlist that we created for our road trip out to California. I don't
know why I haven't deleted it yet. God, we were so excited (little did we
know, ha!). Remember how much fun we had on the way out
there? Stopping every few hours to simply take pictures so that we
could prove to our friends that we had, in fact, been
to Fayetteville, Arkansas. And the poor cat, trapped in that carrier the
whole time. We were so worried he'd never make it to California.

For our trip you had created that horrible playlist of music by
Madonna, Britney Spears and of course your favorite, Celine Dion. And
wouldn't you know it, just the other day as I walking down the street
"I Drove All Night" came on my iTunes. Remember when you used
to sing that (badly) at karaoke? I never understood the lyrics to that song.
"I drove all night, to get to you. Is that alright?" Well, what fucking
difference does it make if she drove all night? By the time she got
there, whoever she was driving to see would be like: "hey, you drove all
night, come in, take a load off". One way or the other, I have a feeling it
would be alright that she showed up.

I know I shouldn't have done this, but I looked at
your Instagram profile the other day and I saw that you had deleted all of
the pictures of us that you had on there. That was very hurtful, I must say.
Considering our relationship started before Instagram was even a thing,

that's a lot of memories to get rid of. I also saw that you changed your relationship status to single on Facebook a while back. So I guess the world knows now that we are no longer together. Believe me, the day that you did that I got no less than forty text messages from people I hadn't heard from in years asking if I was OK and saying that "I'll get over it". I hate when people tell me to get over things. Like, if it were that easy no one would ever be sad. If the Allies had said, "Hey Hitler, Jews aren't so bad, stop killing them. Get over it." There would have been no Holocaust. Unfortunately, life does not work like that. I am still very much "under" this. It's been forty-three days. I don't know how long it's going to take for me to move on from this, but I certainly know that at this point forty-three days just isn't going to do it.

I can't believe that we haven't spoken over the phone since we broke up. It just seems weird to me. We spoke every single day, relentlessly, for ten years and the only correspondence we've had in the past few weeks is via email and the occasional text. Yes, I know we aren't together anymore and yes, I know that that's not what people who aren't in a relationship anymore do, but don't you think it's been weird? I mean, we had the same routine of talking, texting and seeing each other every day and now it's gone. It's like I've lost my best friend.

I honestly hope that you've thought a little bit about us and haven't completely moved on. I take responsibility for my end, which was a lot, and I really think that we can move forward from this and grow as a couple and be even better than we were before. I remember when we met and you were just a shy young girl who barely spoke two words to me. Before I knew it, you couldn't stop talking to me. You always told me that I was the reason that you were able to come out of your shell because I was so easy to talk to. That I was the person who gave you the ability to finally be you because I didn't give a fuck and was never bothered by anything you did. Remember the good times? I made you feel better than anyone else ever did. Remember that?

Anyway, in the past few weeks I have been a laundry folder, a cleaning man, a flyer hander-outer, a busboy, a dishwasher, a cater waiter and dog walker. My computer broke about two weeks back, so I haven't been able to send out resumes so no one has really gotten back to me about full time employment. I can't even write my weekly articles because I can't afford to fix my computer and pay rent and eat. God I wish we had never moved to California. It literally ruined our lives.

I'd love to hear back from you. I am ready to talk about this whenever you are.

I love you,
Max

From: Gretchen Edwards
To: Max Roberts
RE: This Made Me Think of You
November 04, 2014 at 3:19 PM

Hi Max —

It's great to hear from you. I'm sorry it took me so long to respond, but in about a month I begin my extensive traveling of the country for work so prepping for that and dealing with my every day affairs here has been quite taxing.

I erased our pictures off of Instagram because it hurt me too much to look at them. I didn't mean it as a malicious tactic. I still have everything saved on my computer, so nothing is gone forever. I will always cherish the many memories that we have together. But remember, I am going through a breakup as well. You have to remember that. It was very hard for me to look on my Instagram, or any social media page for that matter, and see pictures of the two of us together. I must say I am a bit taken aback by the fact that you take responsibility for me coming out of my shell. We were twenty when we met. We are thirty now. Yes, you certainly were the more outgoing one of us when we met, but in the ten years we were together I changed a lot. It's called: your twenties. You grow and become the person who you're meant to be in your twenties. Don't give yourself so much credit, Max.

Listen, I appreciate your apologies, I really do. And I feel terrible for the financial situation you are in right now. I am making a bit more money than I was when we were together so if you need money, please let me know. You know I would do anything for you.

Let's grab coffee soon,
Gretchen

From: Max Roberts
To: Gretchen Edwards
RE: This Made Me Think of You
November 04, 2014 at 6:17 PM

Gretchen –

I wasn't emailing you because I wanted money, I was emailing you because about a month ago you said that you needed space and I was giving it to you. I had thought that this was enough time for you to have space and to regroup so that you could get your things together before traveling began.

I would love to grab coffee with you. Just say the word and I will be there.

Love,
Max

Text exchange:

November 06, 2014

Max: Coffee? Tomorrow after work? (12:14 PM)
Gretchen: Sure. Our usual spot? (12:26 PM)
Max: See you at 6? (12:27 PM)
Gretchen: Perfect. (READ: 12:46 PM)

Text exchange:

November 07, 2014

Max: Hey, it's 6:30. I'm at Lalo. Where are you? (6:30 PM)
Gretchen: Shit. I'm sorry, Max. I'm just getting out of work. Are you still there? (7:48 PM)
Max: No. I'm home. (7:49 PM)
Gretchen: Can I make it up to you? Can I take you to dinner tomorrow night? (7:50 PM)
Max: No. Sorry. I am organizing some woman's home and she said she'd need me all night. I really need the money. Another time? (READ: 9:35 PM)

From: Gretchen Edwards
To: Max Roberts
RE: This Made Me Think of You
November 14, 2014 at 11:18 AM

Max –

I am so sorry about last week. I really am. I have been completely swamped at work and with Black Friday coming up and a new line coming out in February, things got out of hand. I truly did not mean to stand you up. You know I have never done that before and you know how much you mean to me. I'm sorry.

I think it's time that we did speak face-to-face to be honest. I have reread that angry email that you sent me the day I broke up with you every day since and every time I read it, it makes me hate you a little bit. I really am trying to get over it, but it's hard as you said so many hurtful things to me. You told me that California was in fact my fault and that I was basically the cause of all of your strife and financial woes. I know deep down that you don't mean that, I really do, but you must understand how hurtful that is to hear and see. I don't know why I read that email every day. I think it's to remind myself of how bad things really can get with you and I don't know if I want to put myself in that position again. Yes, you did make me feel like the most special and important person in the room every time we were together, there is no denying that. But there is also no denying the fact that when you were mad, you made me feel like trash. You made me feel horrible. There were times when we were in California that you made me think that I wasn't good enough and there were times when you made me want to kill myself. I never told you because you were in such a bad place over there, but it's true – you did. Your actions and your words mean more than you think. I was hurting over there too and you never asked how I was because you were so concerned about becoming the next big, hot shot writer in Hollywood. You never asked about me and I was sitting right in front of you.

Having said that, there were two people in this relationship, or whatever the saying is. I was at fault for a lot of things and there are a lot of things that I did that were unforgiveable. I am sorry for my part in this. After all of these exchanges, I just realized that I never said I was sorry. Max, I don't want you to think that this is all on you. Things got too complicated, we were always in survival mode and we didn't know how to handle our feelings. I know that couples have financial issues and fights all of the time and seem to work it out somehow, but it went on for so long that I didn't feel things could ever be worked out. I was afraid that the way we were in California and when we returned to New York was how it was going to be forever and I needed to find a way out. Yes, I remember the good times. How could I not? But the good times seem so far behind us that it seems impossible to me that I would be able to move forward with you and not always have my guard up. When I said I wasn't in love with you a few weeks back, I was just saying that to be mean. It's not completely true and I apologize for that as well. A part of me will always be very deeply in love with you and I think that deep down inside you know that.

I know you are going through a hard time and I know that I am partly at fault for it, but I promise you things will get better. I mean what I said. Dinner -- my treat whenever you want. I am leaving for a month in Cleveland (how that shit hole ended up being my first stop, I will never know) on December 1st, but will be back on the weekends and will hopefully be a little less stressed. Maybe we can get together then? It is weird not seeing you, I agree. Maybe if we take things super slow we can try to work them out? How is the cat? I miss Robert so much.

Love,
Gretchen

From: Max Roberts
To: Gretchen Edwards
RE: This Made Me Think of You
November 15, 2014 at 8:04 AM

Gretchen –

Robert is good. I have to say looking at him makes me think of you sometimes (and when I say sometimes, I basically mean all the time). I wonder if you had the right idea in abandoning him with me so that you wouldn't have to see him every day, but I'd never give him away and love him to pieces. I'm sure he would say "hi" if he could.

I appreciate the dinner invitation, but I think I may have to pass on that for now. I've been really busy with my many part time jobs and I never really know when it's possible for me to take off. When we made plans to meet and you didn't show up, I lost out on a gig that would have paid at least half my rent and as much as I want to see you, I can't afford to do that again.

I was hoping to get the key to our storage unit from you last week when we were supposed to have coffee, but you never showed. I called the facility to see if they would allow me in, but yours is the only name on the lease and unless I come with the key, they won't let me enter. Would you mind sending me the key? I really need to get my things as it's getting colder and all of my winter clothes are in there. My address is at the end of the email.

You don't have to apologize for anything, sweetheart. I understand where you are coming from. I regret writing that angry letter to you after we broke up. That's why I started writing you letters about things that made me think of you. I thought that that way you could see the happy memories and thoughts that I had about us and try to forget about the bad. I assumed it's easier for you to try and remember the bad things and to push the good times we had out of your memories. That way your decision seems easier to bear. Please erase that email. I never should have written it in the first place and I already apologized. How much longer can we go back and forth about the same things? Please try to move on.

I'm sorry I can't meet you for dinner. Don't get me wrong, I really want to, but I've also been under the weather (and can't take off work) and I don't want to get you sick. Especially not before your big journey begins.

Gretchen, I love you. I am so happy that you are thinking that you may want to try and work things out with me. It means so much.

Max.

134 West 159th Street. Apt. 4D
NY, NY 10032

xo

From: Gretchen Edwards
To: Max Roberts
RE: This Made Me Think of You
November 16, 2014 at 8:59 AM

I'm sorry that you were under the weather, but you honestly should have let me known that all of your winter clothes were in storage. I had absolutely no idea that you weren't allowed in without a key. I could have sworn that I put your name on the lease.

I had my assistant Amanda rush to your apartment to drop off the key for the unit as soon as I got your email yesterday. She said that when she got there and handed you the key that you were very surprised to see her as I imagine you would be. She said that your clothes were practically threadbare and you hadn't shaved. She said that you looked sickly. Is something going on over there that I need to know about? I checked your Instagram account but you haven't posted a selfie since we were in California. Amanda said you looked nothing like that picture. I know I should have told you that Amanda was coming over, but you said that you weren't feeling well and I wanted to make sure that you could get your things from storage as quickly as possible. Please let me know that you are OK.

Anyway, I don't mean to browbeat you. I hope that you were able to get into the unit without a problem. You know if you need anything, I am always going to be here for you. Just ask.

Gretchen.

From: Max Roberts
To: Gretchen Edwards
RE: This Made Me Think of You
November 17, 2014 at 9:01 AM

Gretchen –

I'm sorry; I didn't think that someone would be personally coming over to drop the key off, so when Amanda knocked on my door it was super unexpected. I thought you would simply throw the key in the mail. You really didn't need to send her but thank you so much for making the effort.

Truthfully, I am not in much of a state to see anyone. As I said in earlier exchanges, I didn't have any winter clothes so the clothes I do have have become a bit worn over the past few months. I didn't want to pester you with my needs so I didn't push to get the key for our storage unit from you because I knew you were busy and didn't want to bother. With the move to California and trying to acclimate back to life in New York, my expenses have been through the roof and unfortunately, I haven't been able to spend the little extra money I have on new clothes. I hope your assistant wasn't revolted by my appearance. Embarrassingly, I had to borrow a coat from a guy in AA because I was so cold and my clothes were so worn that I was catching cold every time I walked out the door. I also haven't been able to afford hair gel or razors and I haven't gotten a hair cut in over two months so I am looking a bit worse for the wear lately, hence my unshaved appearance the other day. I definitely don't look like my last Instagram selfie anymore, that's for sure. I can't afford a gym membership nowadays and can only afford but one meal a day; so unfortunately, my strong physique is no longer. I'm a wet noodle now. I just look like shit and I didn't want to be seen by a stranger. Honest, I wasn't expecting someone from your office or I would have tried to make myself a bit more presentable.

Thank you, however, for giving me the key. I got to go down to the unit this morning and get all of my clothes back here via subway. People must have thought that I was homeless. I didn't realize how much stuff we had in there. I guess when you are going through a transition like this, you kind of forget about the material things. It's a wonder I have lived the way that I have over the past few months. I really don't have much and it doesn't seem to bother me in the slightest, not like it used to. I could have -- if the weather hadn't changed -- lived out of that single duffle bag that I brought here for weeks to come. I guess I really am beginning to realize that none of this material shit matters much anymore. You and my other loved ones are what matters to me. I will have a few extra bucks next week so I was going to shave and maybe work out at the Y where I go to my AA meetings.

I barely recognize myself, to be honest. When I was in storage, I found a framed picture of us from the night that my second book came out. Remember that party? I bought you that slinky, black cocktail dress. Man, you looked like a million bucks. Hey, I did too, in that tux! (Then to make you feel better while I was on tour, I got you a tuxedo cat to keep you company while I was away. Robert says "hi," by the way). We were so God damned happy. At the time, you were just an assistant and look at you now. Now you're running an entire department of a fashion brand and traveling across the country to every store to make sure their women's wear line is being properly represented. I am so proud of you. I looked at the picture of us and then I looked at myself in the mirror. Several years later, I look and feel like a completely different person. I suppose I am a different person then I was two years ago. My hair is gross. It used to be so perfectly manicured. I was always a slicked back blond. My skin is awful. I have bags under my eyes because I can't ever sleep. What I wouldn't do to have a time machine that could take us back two years. Life would be perfect again. And I'd look so much better! I'm sure you still look ravishing!

I know this sounds fucking bananas, but I think about you every day.

Max.

From: Gretchen Edwards
To: Max Roberts
RE: This Made Me Think of You
November 18, 2014 at 4:44 PM

Max –

It's not bananas. I still think of you often as well.

I didn't realize you were in such a state. I really am only making a few more thousand dollars a year here than I was back in Los Angeles, but if you need anything, let me know. Scratch that, the second I finish this email, I am just going to Venmo you some cash so you have it on hand. You shouldn't be walking around the city with nothing in your pocket.

I would still love to get together. Are you still going to AA meetings? You haven't spoken much about them in the past few emails. I know it's weird that we haven't spoken after all this time, but I promise you, we will get together very soon.

I'm going to send you that money now. Spend it wisely.

Gretchen.

Tweet:

November 23, 2014:

@maxrobertsauthor: "Spending Thanksgiving hitting the gym and getting back in shape. Happy holiday to all!"

Facebook:

Dec 01, 2014 at 4:16 PM:

Check-in: Gretchen Edwards is in Cleveland, Ohio.
"Cleveland...er...rocks?!"

From: Max Roberts
To: Gretchen Edwards
RE: This Made Me Think of You
December 02, 2014 at 6:17 PM

Gretchen --

I never received that Venmo money that you said you were going to give me. I really appreciate you offering to help, I really do. You have, in fact, said that you were going to help several times and haven't. I don't want you to think that I am only reaching out to you because I need money, because that is certainly not the case. But have a little respect for me. If you don't want to help that's completely fine. But don't say you are going to do something and not do it. It's very disrespectful.

I didn't respond to your last email for two weeks because I called you twice and you didn't pick up, so I was under the impression that you didn't want to speak to me. I don't know what is going on with you, but it's really hurting my feelings, to be honest.

I am still going to AA every day, thank you for asking. Sometimes it helps, sometimes it does not. If nothing else, it kills an hour of my day. I really haven't craved a drink since that night I texted you that I thought I was going to drink, so I guess I've been alright, but the sadness is still there. I didn't bring it up, because you were pissed at me, but you missed my sobriety date in October. It's the first time in eight years that I haven't gotten a call or a text or a hug from you in celebration of that day. It was truly upsetting to think that you had forgotten what was once such an important day for us.

I am really disappointed in how things have turned out between us. I still want us to get back together, but something has changed over the last two and half months. I guess it's distance and the fact that we haven't seen each other face to face but with every day that passes, I begin to think that you forget about me more and more. You said that you lied when you told me that you weren't in love with me anymore but I'm not sure how much of a lie that really was. You stood me up, you didn't send money when you said you were going to and you don't ever seem to want to pick up the damn phone when I call. Moreover, and not to harp on the past, but it's very hard for me to understand how after ten years you could break up with me over the phone and think nothing of it. You said over the phone, "people get divorced all the time, you'll get through this". I understand that, but I think before most people get divorced they at least make some sort of attempt to work it out. Counseling, therapy, giving each other a chance, something, I don't know. This has all been very hurtful, Gretchen. I need you to know that.

I was really hurt when you didn't show up at Lalo the night that we were supposed to have coffee a few weeks back because I had a little surprise for you. Since my planned marriage proposal fell on deaf ears, I decided to do something else that I thought would be equally romantic, but you weren't around to see it. Remember when we were juniors in college and started dating? You were so content with me at the time and how I had helped you come out of your shell that you were going to rebel against your parents and get a tattoo. I took you to downtown Baltimore to that seedy place in Fells Point, gave the tattoo artist two-hundred bucks and told him to do whatever you wanted. And you asked for that horrible tree on your back! I stood by and didn't say a word during the five hours it took him to finish that tattoo, but I held your hands and smiled as you were in pain to show my solidarity. Afterwards, your back in a bloody disarray, you turned to me and said "your turn" and I laughed in your face. There was no way I was ever going to get a tattoo and you knew it. For years you asked me if I wanted to go with you and get matching tattoos with our initials and I always refused. Well, the night before we were supposed to meet for coffee, I finally took the plunge and got your initials tattooed on the inside of my arm. A nice little *G.E.*, in cursive. A friend of mine is a tattoo artist and said he'd do it for free, so I bit the bullet and just did it. It was almost like an unconscious decision. I don't know what came over me that night. I didn't get it because I wanted to use it as a ploy to try and get you back or anything like that. I got it because I really wanted you to see that this relationship is forever to me. I am changing all of things that you didn't like about me and I realize the error of my ways. I am changing so much, in fact, that I went and got a tattoo with your initials in my arm because I knew it was something that you really wanted once and thought that I would never do it. That way, with your initials on my inner arm, you're always by my side and close to my heart.

You say all of these things -- that you're going to help, that you're hurting too, that you still love me, but there's no follow through on any of it. It seems as though I am the only one doing any of the work. You said you need to work on yourself, but you won't exactly tell me what you're doing and it seems, through social media, that all you're really doing is going out and partying. I know you are the one who broke up with me, but can't I get a little credit for fighting as hard as I am? Quite honestly (and I know it seems very pathetic) I have never seen or heard of anyone fighting for someone as hard as I have and gotten so little in response.

Just to fill you in: I am working at Macy's all month so I will be really busy too. I was hired as extra holiday help this year and I really do need the cash so I don't know how much I will be around -- I know you aren't around much either these days since you're traveling for work, but maybe we can finally catch up or talk on the phone. Either is up to you. I really would love to hear your voice at the very least.

Please don't think I am mad at you about the money, I am really not. It just bothered me, that's all, and I really wanted to get that off my chest so it didn't come up later in another exchange.

Love,
Max

To: Max Roberts
From: Gretchen Edwards
RE: This Made Me Think of You
December 06, 2014 at 7:17 AM

Max –

I had a nightmare and it scared me to my core. I dreamt that we were back in California and that I had gotten pregnant with your child and had an abortion. I woke up in a cold sweat. I hate to say this to you over email because it's very inappropriate, but this dream struck me because I did, in fact, have an abortion when we were living in California that I never told you about it.

We were bickering so much and paying so little attention to each other at the time that that one night we had sex (remember, when you came in so excited because you thought you had gotten a writing job – which didn't turn out to be anything – and we had a nice dinner out, the one and only time we ever did that in California). I had forgotten to take my birth control pill for so long because we weren't having sex regularly and a few weeks later ended up pregnant. I didn't tell you because you hadn't gotten the gig that you thought you had and were so upset over it that I didn't want to make you even more upset. Honestly, we were in no position to have a child at the time and I made the decision alone and didn't tell you because I truly thought it was the right choice to make. There was no possible way for us to care for a child and with our financials being the way they were, we couldn't afford one either. This really played into my breaking up with you because I have been so racked with guilt over this since it happened. I hope that you can forgive me for this. I honestly did this to try and save our relationship, as fucked up as that sounds, but I know you may never understand that. It is quite possibly one of the worst things I could have ever done to you, but I felt backed into a corner and didn't think I had a choice. I wanted to tell you so many times, on the car ride back from California where we basically didn't speak the entire five days and after we got back to New York, but then we broke up and I didn't feel that it was appropriate for me to bring up. I know it's classless to do this via email, but I needed you to know.

I'm also sorry about the money. I didn't mean to not send it. After I emailed you, Amanda came in and started rattling off a list of things I needed to do for my boss and I just lost track of time. Every time you called after that, I was in meetings. I don't want you to think I'm a big to-do but my plate has been really full lately and I know that's not an excuse, but sometimes I feel like it's a bit more than I can handle. If you still need money, please let me know. I'm happy to give it to you – I don't have a lot but what's yours is mine.

I will reach out to you when I am back in town this weekend.

Gretchen.

Dec. 06, 2014 4:57 PM

Missed Call: Max (28)

To: Gretchen Edwards
From: Max Roberts
RE: This Made Me Think of You
December 07, 2014 at 6:19 AM

Gretchen –

I honestly cannot believe that you would tell me such a thing over email and then have the audacity to ignore my phone calls. You are not the woman I thought you are. Don't get me wrong, I would have absolutely told you to go through with an abortion, one hundred percent. You're right, we were in a tough spot and in no position to have a child, but honest to God, don't you think I at least had the right to know that I had fathered a child? Don't you think it's a bit unfair of you to make a decision like that without me? What's worse is that for the past two and a half months, I have relentlessly apologized for the things that I have done wrong and you drop the bombshell the size of Hiroshima and won't even pick up the damn phone when I call. You have quite the nerve to sit and berate me over and over again with my wrongdoings and faults when you can't even come clean about quite possibly the worst thing I have ever heard anyone do to someone they supposedly love and care for.

I also don't understand why you refuse to respond to the messages that I actually send you. I was going to propose. I got your fucking initials tattooed on my arm. Why doesn't this seem to make any difference to you? You keep telling me that you want to try to move on, and yet nothing I seem to ever say makes any difference to you.

Please. I am not asking for a lot. I am simply asking for a response that fits the delivered message and at this point, it's the least you can fucking do.

Max.

From: Gretchen Edwards
To: Max Roberts
RE: This Made Me Think of You
December 07, 2014 at 10:59 AM

Max --

What I did was wrong and it's completely understandable if you can't forgive me. I'm sorry, but things when I found out that I was pregnant were not good. We had just moved to California and your mood had changed so drastically that the thought of bringing someone else into the equation seemed incomprehensible. Yes, it was great driving out to California and yes, we had fun for about the first two days we were there, but once things settled down and the reality that things weren't going to magically fall in to place the way you wanted them to set in, you turned into a different person. Living with you was kind of unbearable. I know, I know, it's not who you are, but at the time, having a child was unthinkable. I didn't do it to betray you; I did it because I felt it was the right thing to do. We had no money. We were miserable. I felt that I had no other options. Yes, I know that not telling you until after the fact was wrong (and doing it via email was even worse) but I didn't want you to get the idea in your head that a baby was going to save our relationship. You had no job, we could barely afford the place we lived in at that point and we were fighting every day. This was around the time of my birthday when we had so little money that we literally laid in bed all day and did nothing but watch Netflix. It was the most depressing birthday I've ever had. I know that that's not entirely your fault, but I had to do what I thought was best. I know it was wrong to not include you in this decision but I felt that I had no choice.

As far as everything else is concerned, Max, come on. Your relentless begging and pleading doesn't make me want to get back together with you. It doesn't remind me of the good old days, it reminds me of why I stopped wanting to be with you in the first place. I appreciate your tenacity but I was speaking to Claire about this the other day (she and Bruce are finally pregnant, if you want to send her a note) and she told me that after Bruce and her broke up for that little bit a few years ago, it wasn't until she stopped begging him to come back that he finally took her back. Hearing you tell me that you were going to propose and that you got my initials tattooed in your arm are very flattering things -- I truly mean it -- but if you were to act a little more cool, calm and collected, it may help me remember the good times and not reflect so much on the bad. I know you are trying but maybe if you stopped trying so hard, it would help me appreciate you a little bit more. I'm not trying to be a bitch, but it seems as though every time we take a step forward, you do something that sends us hurtling seven steps back. I know the revelation of an abortion doesn't help my case, but you have to see things from my point of view. Just take it easy and maybe after the New Year we can get together.

I still love you Max, but this is too much. Please relax and let's try to get together after the 1st.

Gretchen

Text exchange:

December 07, 2014

Max: I just got your email, you have some nerve Gretchen. (11:45 AM)
Gretchen: Cool down, Max. Let's talk about this in a few weeks. (11:46 AM)
Max: Cool down? Seriously?" (11:48 AM)
Gretchen: Yes, this year has been stressful for us both. I'm sorry for what I did, but you have to understand where I am coming from. (11:49 AM)
Max: I do. What pisses me off is the fact that you have blamed me for everything that has gone wrong in this relationship when your side of the street is far from clean. You've barely apologized for having an abortion behind my back and I have relentlessly apologized for calling you names and being mean. One of these things is clearly not like the other. (11:51 AM)
Gretchen: I am sorry, Max. I thought I explained myself in the emails. (11:52 AM)
Max: Whatever. (11:52 AM)
Gretchen: I'm sorry, I'm really busy. Can we please talk about this another time? (11:53 AM)
Max: Why bother? You won't pick up your phone anyway. (READ: 11:54 AM)

From: Max Roberts
To: Gretchen Edwards
RE: This Made Me Think of You
December 09, 2014 at 11:39 PM

Gretchen –

I can't sleep. I've been tossing and turning for about an hour now and all I can think about is the baby we could have had. Again, not that I wanted it or think it would have done anything to save our relationship or make us happier in any way, but the fact that you felt you couldn't tell me that you were pregnant in the first place has really struck a chord. What the hell happened to us that got us to that place? We used to be able to tell each other everything. Even when we were in California I still told you everything: how I was hurting, how I felt like a failure, how I wished we had never left New York in the first place. No matter what happened, I was always honest with you and I never, ever lied to you or betrayed you and I certainly didn't do things that could have potentially affected your future behind your back.

Again, I do understand why you did what you did. I would have told you to do the same. It's the simple fact that you felt the need to make this decision without even factoring me into the equation that disappoints me so deeply. What's more, you've taken every opportunity to tell me how harshly I treated you, which you're right was unfair. However, those were words, words that I apologized for saying time and time again. I don't fully understand how you can be so mad at me for the words I said when you took an action that was so hurtful and disrespectful. It seems as though the power of my words outweighs your actions and if that's truly something you believe then I guess we don't really know each other at all anymore.

The holidays are coming up and it's been incredibly difficult without you here, but with this latest revelation I have decided to really work on myself – to start writing again, really focus on working out again and start putting the focus back on me and taking it off of us. My fruitless efforts to try and get you back have been a waste of time and have gotten me nowhere. I think you are right and I think we do need a break from speaking. These hurtful exchanges aren't making me feel better and are just prolonging the inevitable and I am sure you feel the same. I hope you have a wonderful holiday and a very happy new year.

Max

From: Max Roberts
To: Gretchen Edwards
RE: This Made Me Think of You
December 25, 2014 at 10:59 PM

Gretchen –

Merry Christmas.

I just wanted to reach out and say hello. It's so weird not spending Christmas with you. I don't even know where you are, although I assume you've gone down to Baltimore to spend some time with your family. I hope you're having a lovely time.

I spent my morning at the gym (I'm really getting back into great shape) and then had an early dinner with Brett and some of my buddies from AA then went to work at Macy's. I really tried not to celebrate the holidays this year because it makes me think of you.

I always made such a production out of Christmas every year. I always got us a tree, always showered you with gifts and always tried so hard to make it a special day for you. My favorite memories of Christmases past are how you'd always know just the right gift to give me. I'd open it and be so happy to receive it and you'd always question me relentlessly with "is this OK? Did I get the right thing?". You always did. You always knew just what to give me.

As I sit in my apartment and type this email to you, watching Robert high on the catnip I gave him for Christmas in the corner, I can't help but think of our last Christmas together in our old apartment, before we moved to California. You, me and the cat were so happy and so hopeful about our impending move to California. The thought honestly strikes me deep in my soul and to be honest, it's been all I've thought about all month. How happy we were and what a bad decision we made in moving and how you aren't with me this year.

I've been trying to pray – to be more spiritual. It's a very important part of AA, but for some reason all I can do is pray to go back in time or pray that you'll come back to me. It's not the right way to pray. You're not supposed to pray for things you want but somehow that's all I can do. I need to get a better handle on my spirituality (or at least my sponsor thinks I need to).

I just couldn't celebrate Christmas this year without you. I just couldn't do it.

Max

Facebook:

December 27, 2014 at 9:16 AM

Max Roberts: "Happy birthday to me!"

Facebook:

December 30, 2014 at 5:19 PM

Gretchen Edwards: "New Year's in Vegas with my bitches!"

From: Max Roberts
To: Gretchen Edwards
RE: This Made Me Think of You
January 03, 2015 at 7:18 PM

Gretchen --

This was the first time in so many years that I didn't hear from you on my birthday. It just wasn't the same. I actually had a great time with Brett and some of my AA buddies. We went to Carmine's for dinner (a tradition you started eight years ago and I am happy to report, lives on to this day) and ate so much Italian food that I thought I was going to burst at the seams. I really have found a great group of friends in AA and they have helped so much in getting me through the hard times, especially the holidays which have been particularly lonely since I couldn't go home to see my father of Natalie because I had to work at Macy's.

On my birthday, I couldn't help but think of you. You always had a special way of making me feel like the most important person in the world. Especially my twenty-fourth birthday when you threw that surprise party for me and called all of our friends back for the holidays with their families to celebrate with us on the roof top of the Standard Hotel. I will never, ever forget how much fun we had that night. You asked me that year if I wanted anything for my birthday and I said that all I wanted was you, forever. That's still all I want. I understand that you feel the need to focus on all of the bad things that happened between the two of us. I think it helps you deal with some of the choices you've made over the last year and I am sure that I would do the same if I was in your position. I have tried to do the same. However, this time of year it is difficult not to think of the happier times.

I get what you are saying about laying low, which is why I haven't reached out since our last exchange. I saw on your Facebook that you were in Vegas with the girls. I hope you got to see Britney Spears finally, since I refused to go with you for all of these years. Remember our first New Year's together? We went to that horrible party near Camden Yards, then I drove you back to your dorm in that shitty Ford Fiesta that I had in college. Remember how that car always smelled like a wet dog even though I never had a dog? Weird. That was the first night that you told me that you loved me. You were so nervous to tell me and cried afterwards saying "I shouldn't have said it, but I wanted to tell you how I felt". Then I didn't respond and you started to cry even more. You were so sweet and innocent back then. I feel like I had a part in ruining that innocence but I can't help but remember that girl, so timid and shy, reaching out with a declaration of love and me being a dick and not telling you I loved you as well until a few weeks later (over the phone, no less). I sometimes think about that night and it makes me smile so much. You flipped out after you told me that you loved me because you had never said it to anyone else and thought it was too soon. Then you were like "you might as well just break up with me because I am a basket case", and I laughed. Little did you know, I felt exactly the same way. God, I love that memory of you. That's how I like to remember our relationship.

I saved up enough money from working at Macy's this holiday season to get my computer fixed so I've been writing again and I must say it's been very cathartic. I don't know if my publisher will even want to buy another book from me, but writing has always helped me feel better and right now I am trying to do whatever it takes to feel better. I'm going to the gym, working on my AA program and trying to be the best me I can be. I still feel sad from time to time but I was told by many people in the program that I am doing everything I possibly can, but I still can't help but feel the way I feel. Heartbreak does take some time to move past. I am starting to feel much better about life and I hope you are too.

Hope to hear from you soon,
Max.

Text Exchange:

January 03, 2015

Gretchen: Shit! Max. I wrote you a happy birthday text and forgot to press send. I'm a mess. Got your email, running through the airport to catch a fight. Hope you're well. XO. (10:39 PM)
Gretchen: Flight, not fight. Jeez. (10:39 PM)
Max: No worries. Safe travels. (READ: 10:40 PM)

From: Max Roberts
To: Gretchen Edwards
RE: This Made Me Think of You
January 16, 2015 at 4:56 PM

Hi Gretchen –

Have you heard of Tinder? What a weird way of dating. They didn't have these things back when we met. Isn't it weird how much can change in ten years? Ten years ago it was strange when people met online, now everyone is meeting over their phone. It seems so disingenuous. Anyway, I downloaded it onto my phone the other day because I was super bored at Macy's and like sixteen ladies had reached out to me by the time I turned it back on an hour later. It's so odd, all of these women (some of whom aren't even that attractive) have such a large Instagram following. I don't get it. They're OK looking, but it seems to me that they pretend to have far more interesting lives than they do in reality because once I begin speaking to them, they have little to nothing to say. What a waste of time. Social media is so stupid. I check your Instagram account searching for answers as to what you are doing, relentlessly look at who is following you and the pictures you've liked as if it's going to someone uncover what it is that you are up to. It doesn't. It just drives me a little crazy.

I have been hitting the gym a lot lately and getting those endorphins going, so I'm not only feeling better but looking a little bit better. It's kind of nice to get this attention via Tinder, even though I know it doesn't mean much. I haven't really been with anyone since we broke up – I guess I am kind of scared to, which is interesting coming from a guy. You know guys usually just throw themselves back out there after a relationship ends, but I've never been much like other guys. All of my AA buddies keep telling me to go out and try to get laid, but I just can't bring myself to do it. There was this nice looking girl, Sandra, who reached out to me via

Tinder. We had a decent conversation. I think she's Hungarian or something. Maybe I will ask her out for coffee. I don't know.

I have a bit of good news! Brett asked me to move in with him, which is really exciting. He's been having some troubles lately (financial and emotional) and asked if I wanted to take his spare room because his current roommate is moving in with his girlfriend. I am going to move in on the first of February. I think this will be great for me too. I really don't like the place I live in now and neither does the cat because he's stuck in my room all of the time because the other roommates don't want a cat running around the apartment all the time. It's nice and all, but it doesn't feel like home. I have someone else's furniture, I still don't know the people I live with very well and this is the apartment I was in when you broke up with me. Living in New York is so funny. It's got to be the only place in the world where one can bounce from apartment to apartment as effortlessly as one gets coffee in the morning. I'm hoping that I will be able to stay with Brett long term instead of month to month like I am here. He's a really great guy, he loves Robert and I think it's going to work out well.

Everything else for me has been on the up-and-up. I'm full time at Macy's now and I am still writing for that website. Last week, I wrote an article about how guys cope when their girlfriends breakup with them and something like two million people shared it on Facebook. Isn't the stupid? God, the internet is a crazy thing. For some reason, after I shared it, people started sending me death threats. As if I am somehow responsible for all that is wrong with the world, a few women reached out to me and told me that I was sexist and that they were going to find me and torture-kill me or some shit. People have way too much time on their hands. Thank God no one does anything at work anymore, or I suppose no one would have the time to read these articles and send their subsequent death threats. All in the name of selling advertisements, I suppose.

Anyway, I just wanted to catch up. I don't know where you've been, but it would be nice to hear from you. It's been over a month. I know you're traveling and I hope you're being safe and everything is OK.

Max

From: Max Roberts
To: Gretchen Edwards
RE: This Made Me Think of You
January 21, 2015 at 1:28 PM

Gretchen –

Two months ago you said that we were going to get together after the first and now January is almost over. Where have you been? I'm starting to feel a little slighted. Again, you have said something that you had no intention of following through with and now my feelings are hurt again. Listen, if you think I am still mad about the abortion, I am not. I have really been working on my program and I have forgiven you for what you did. Honest, I have. I don't want that to hold you back from contacting me. You did what you felt you had to do. My feelings were hurt, but I've let it go and won't bring it up again.

Sometimes I think (and I'm not trying to sound like an asshole when I say this) that I had more of a reason to break up with you than you did with me and I have completely forgiven you for everything that you did to me. I yelled at you because I was in a bad place. We fought because we had no money. Couples fight about money and call each other names and as much as it sucks, it's a harsh reality of being in an adult relationship. You had an abortion behind my back and I've still managed to forgive you. I feel that if I can forgive you for that, then you can certainly forgive me for having a few bad months and move on. Not only that, I feel that you've taken this "time to make yourself feel better and get over it" at my expense. You've gone out and had your fun while I have really taken this as an opportunity to work on myself and still have a slight hope that we can manage to work this out. I don't understand why you can't find it in your heart to move on with me – you have kind of put me through emotional hell. I get why you feel the way you feel, but if you think I am unable to get past the abortion thing (I know I said I got over things in the past and brought them up again, but this time I really mean it) it's simply not true. I get it.

I know I was mean in California and when we got back, but honestly, I have done everything that I said I was going to do and you've been all talk. You haven't even responded to me in almost two months. It's confusing.

Max

From: Max Roberts
To: Gretchen Edwards
RE: This Made Me Think of You
January 28, 2015 at 9:27 PM

Gretchen –

Did you know that when you are walking over the George Washington Bridge as a pedestrian, there is no guard rail to prevent you from jumping off? Isn't that the most ridiculous thing you've ever heard? I mean, you're so high up when you're walking across it and thousands of people tread that path every day. I guess Brett knew this because two nights ago he walked halfway across it and jumped off. Apparently, he went out and got drunk, did a bunch of coke and decided to kill himself. I knew that he was having troubles, and I think that was one of the reasons that he had reached out to me and asked me to move in, but I had no idea that his troubles were this bad. Police found his body on the shore of Riverside Park. They could barely identify him. The river was so cold that he was practically frozen when he washed ashore. When they took him in for an autopsy, they found several substances in his system, one of which I am assuming was cocaine because I know from meetings that he used to do a lot of coke back in his using days. I wish I could have helped him. I knew he was going through some tough times, but I had no idea that things were this bad because he never really told me. I feel terrible for not being there for him.

I talked to Chuck, another friend from AA, about this last night over the phone. Chuck isn't someone I confide in much – he was more of Brett's friend – but he told me that Brett was having some serious financial issues and was apparently having an affair with this girl who came to him about a week ago and told him that she was pregnant and needed money. When he asked her to take a paternity test, she refused and he began to think that she was just bilking him for cash. Chuck told me that Brett was tortured over all of these things and because of his BPD and alcoholism, it consumed him. He fell off the wagon then jumped off a bridge.

The funeral is set for next week. His parents are coming up from South Carolina to make all of the final arrangements tomorrow night. I can't imagine what they are going through. The really fucked up part of all of this is that I know that Brett was really trying so hard. He went to meetings every day, he had a great fellowship, he always spoke (or I thought he did) openly about his feelings and yet he built up all of this sadness behind closed doors. This disease is so fucked up and scary. Alcoholism is just the worst and I know from what I go through on a daily basis in order to stay sober how hard it is. I, luckily, can cope with it (sometimes) but others aren't so fortunate. It's a desperate situation for some and unfortunately so many stories end like Brett's.

I'm in pain. I got through my mother's death and I have no doubt that I can be strong through this as well. Death is a part of life. This whole situation has made me think of you and how you handled my mother's death with such grace and elegance. I have to get something off my chest today as well. I suppose I need to make another amends to you, something that I should have told you last summer but didn't. When we got back from California and I went down to Baltimore to see my father for the night, I had an experience similar to Brett's, but luckily not the same fate. After my father went to bed that night, I went into his garage and found an old pistol that he hid in a cigar box that he thought Natalie and I never knew about, but always did. I loaded the gun and put it to my head. I was so lost when we got back from California. We were fighting so much and I had turned into such a greedy, evil monster and I knew I had turned you away from me. I wanted to kill myself, but couldn't pull the trigger. I thought of you and what you would have to deal with if I had committed suicide. I'm also terribly frightened of death. I know everyone eventually dies, but I was too scared to do it myself. California killed me long before I ever contemplated committing suicide so there was no point. When I got back to New York after my visit with my father, you broke up with me the next day. Part of me wonders if it would have just been smarter for me to end it then and there. Even though I no longer have you or Brett, I know I could never do that.

I'm so torn up over this. I told the people that I am living with that I am going to stay indefinitely now since Brett is no longer with us. He was such a great guy Gretchen, I really wish you could have met him. I know he had a lot of issues, but he truly was a wonderful friend to me and I am so sorry that you will never get the opportunity to sit and laugh with him because he was a funny son of a bitch.

I really hope that we can get together soon. It would make me feel so much better to see a familiar face. I hope that you are doing well and will reach out soon.

Love,

Max

From: Gretchen Edwards
To: Max Roberts
RE: This Made Me Think of You
January 29, 2015 at 10:04 AM

Max –

I'm so sorry to hear about your friend. How are you holding up? Stupid question, I know. I'm sure you are a mess. I know I would be.

Listen, I know this isn't the best time for me to be telling you this, but it may explain my distance. I've met someone. His name is Larry. Terrible name, I know. He's a friend of Bruce's and is an investment banker who works a lot too, so I don't get to see him a ton (I am still traveling every weekday for work so that doesn't help) but I really like him. He's really funny, smart, attractive and super successful. I thought he was too important or successful to even look twice at me, but I guess I was wrong.

I really hope you aren't mad at me for this. It just happened and I needed to let you know because I couldn't go on much longer not responding to your emails or not being honest about what was going on.

I wasn't expecting this to happen, but it just did. I really was taking this time apart from you to think about our situation and I suppose it just led me to him. I would love for you to meet him sometime, if you're interested. It would be nice to see you.

Gretchen.

From: Max Roberts
To: Gretchen Edwards
RE: This Made Me Think of You
February 03, 2015 at 1:13 PM

Gretchen –

I have been running a lot. Like more than I ever thought I could,
considering the amount of cigarettes I've been smoking recently. After
Brett's funeral yesterday, I put on my running tights and thought it may
be fun to go for a jog, to you know, clear my head and stuff. I was
overwhelmed with grief at the funeral that I just needed to get out of my
own head and I had already been to two AA meetings that day so I
figured, what the fuck? I began my run at 159th and ran down Riverside,
by the park. It was freezing, but the cold helped me keep going. I kept
saying to myself: *if you stop, your sweat will freeze to your body, and
you'll die of frost bite*. I ran past our old apartment in Harlem and just kept
going. I passed Grant's Tomb. Then I passed Columbia. Still, I just kept
running. It was so cold, but I just kept going. Before I knew it, I was at the
Intrepid down on 42nd Street. Didn't stop. Kept going until I hit Chelsea
Piers and could see the lights of the Freedom Tower in front of me. So I
kept going still, not once stopping to catch my breath. Before I knew it, I
had run all the way down to the Brooklyn Bridge. When I got there I
stopped, completely out of breath. For a moment, I contemplated running
to Brooklyn, but quickly decided against it. I looked up at the lights of the
Brooklyn Bridge glowing in the darkness as if there was nothing else
around. It looked like a beckon of hope, a guiding light in the pitch black
darkness that surrounded it. I thought about you and when we first
moved to New York City. How, after we put all of our stuff in our new
apartment, we went straight to the Brooklyn Bridge to take pictures and
act like straight-up tourists. God we had so much fun being stupid
together.

The lights of the Brooklyn Bridge entranced me. I stood there looking at the structure in awe, as if I was living in a world without electricity for years and suddenly seeing this masterpiece that lit up before me, it was as if it was the most spectacular sight I had ever seen. I don't know what came over me. I turned around to enter the subway and realized that I had no money or MetroCard on me. I would have to walk home. It was freezing but I didn't seem to care. I really had nothing else to do anyway.

I walked back up the West Side Highway. I hate the winter in New York after Christmas. It's like we focus so much energy on the holidays for the first part of winter that we forget the weather outside is, in fact, frightful. When all of the stores are decorated with their Christmas lights and Santa Clauses, the cold weather acts almost as a cozy backdrop. Then once all of the decorations come down and you realize everything is dead around you until spring, there's not much to look forward to; it's very sobering and sad. Everyone feels it. It's as cold as fuck, it's hard to get around, no one wants to do anything because they are spent from the holidays and New Year's that you could go until the weather gets better in April before you see a friendly face.

As I continued to walk up the West Side Highway, I saw the lights of the George Washington Bridge in the distance. They were almost blinding in the dark. Uptown is never as bright as it is downtown at night and certain things stick out more than others. I thought of Brett and the terrible time that he must have been going through before he killed himself. I can't imagine what was going through his head at the time, but it must have been bad. That's the thing about suicide. You never really know what people who kills themselves are thinking right before the moment they take the plunge. I hope I never feel like that again. Freezing, I soon found myself running again. I thought my tank was empty, but I suppose it wasn't. I ran, faster than I had before, right to the sidewalk of the George Washington Bridge and looked down. I wanted to get a perspective of what Brett had seen right before he died. For a moment, I thought of jumping myself. Not because I particularly wanted to kill myself, but because I feel like every time people are on top of high bridges or buildings, they think of what it might be like to jump. Or is that just me? I didn't jump, obviously; instead I walked back to my apartment and took a hot shower. All and all I was gone for four hours – in the middle of the night. It really helped me clear my thoughts. I realize Brett did what he thought he needed to do and has hopefully found peace. I am clearly not over losing a friend, but I think I feel a bit better about the situation.

Max

P.S. I figured you were dating someone new. I saw Larry as one of the followers on your Instagram and that he always liked and commented on your pictures and you did the same for him. I never liked Bruce.

From: Max Roberts
To: Gretchen Edwards
RE: This Made Me Think of You
February 04, 2015 at 4:18 PM

Gretchen –

I was in the Duane Reade yesterday and it made me think of you. My legs were so sore from the literal marathon that I had run the night before that I needed some Icy Hot and a heating pad. You know how Duane Reade is always playing "lite-favs" (as I like to call them) from the late 1980s and early 1990s, like Taylor Dayne and Amy Grant, over their loud speaker? Well, yesterday I walked in and they were playing "True Blue" by Madonna. Remember right after we first moved to New York after college and we were unpacking our apartment and you drank an entire bottle of six dollar wine by yourself? We were listening to music and dancing around the apartment like morons and "True Blue" came on and you got up on top of our couch and did a sexy little strip tease but were so drunk that you fell on your ass? We laughed so hard. With the song still playing in the background and you lying on the floor, helpless, I came to your rescue and you whispered: "true blue, baby I love you". And we kissed and made out on the floor for like two hours, completely forgetting that we were supposed to be unpacking, your breath tasting like crappy wine and mine of Doublemint gum and Marlboro Lights. Those were the days, my friend.

It's so weird to call you my friend. I mean, you really are my best friend and the closest person that I have in the city, even though we haven't seen each other in months.

I really hope you have found happiness with this Larry fellow. I hope he's nice to you. AA has helped me a bit in accepting the things that I cannot change and it has become crystal clear that this is something that is beyond my control. When we first broke up, the thought of you with anyone else made me literally ill, but I think I've moved past it. I mean, I'm still not thrilled about it, but it is what it is, I guess.

Love always,

Max

From: Max Roberts
To: Gretchen Edwards
RE: This Made Me Think of You
February 10, 2015 at 6:45 PM

Gretchen –

I have wonderful news!

Remember how I told you that I starting writing again but wasn't expecting anything to come of it? Well, I sent a proposal of an unfinished manuscript to my publisher and they told me that they want to publish it! This is great, considering I thought they had pretty much given up on me after the last one didn't do as well as we had hoped. I'm really excited. I like working at Macy's and writing my little articles and all, but books are really what I was meant to do on this earth. I know I wanted to work in TV for that brief period in California, but I think books are where I belong.

What's really funny about them calling is that they were so impressed with how well I had kept up my social media presence over the years. Even though it has been almost three years since my last book came out, I still had so many Twitter and Facebook followers that they felt it was enough to sell another book. It's so weird that that's how everything works now. If you're popular on social media, you can get a book deal. But, if you think about it, it doesn't mean anything at all. Sure, I have a lot of followers on Facebook, but I don't know them. They have no idea what I have been going through for the past six months, dealing with you and trying to stay sober. It's a presentation of my best self – that's all. It's everyone's best self, but I think social media can bring out the worst in us. Yes, it's nice that this is happening, but I can't help thinking of how I used to look on Instagram and Facebook before we left to go to California and after my last book didn't perform well and think, *wow, I really suck. Everyone else is doing so much better than I am. Why am I such a loser?*

But it's simply not true. No one is doing better than anyone else, ever. Some of us are just better at pretending we are happy on social media than others.

Anyway, I am going off the grid for a bit. I want to really focus on this book and make it count and need to make sure that it's the best that it can be. I think this is really my chance to make something great.

I hope you're well. Have a wonderful Valentine's Day. It always makes me think of you and even if I don't reach out, know that I will be thinking of you and that forty pound box of chocolate I gave you last year when we were in California that we literally ate all in one sitting because we had no money, lol.

Love you,

Max

From: Gretchen Edwards
To: Max Roberts
RE: This Made Me Think of You
February 13, 2015 at 9:02 AM

Max –

What wonderful news! I knew you would have another opportunity to showcase your talents, if you just worked hard for it. I knew you'd never give up! I have no doubt that you will do great work and it will be amazing. I can't wait to find out what you have in store for the world this time around.

Things with me have been OK. The traveling is getting to me. I know it's been only a little over two months being gone every week, but it's certainly taxing on trying to maintain friendships and this budding romance with Larry. In January alone, I was in Austin, Portland, Phoenix, Charleston and Buffalo, coming back to New York in between each stop. I'm really tired and I honestly don't know if I'm cut out for it.

I know I told you that Bruce and Claire are having a baby, but they are due in June and are having a boy. You really should reach out to them and congratulate them. They would be so happy to hear from you.

I hope the writing is going well.

Miss you,

Gretchen

Text exchange:

February 14, 2015

Gretchen: Happy Valentine's Day (READ: 7:45 PM)

From: Gretchen Edwards
To: Max Roberts
RE: This Made Me Think of You
February 19, 2015 at 11:14 AM

Max –

I guess I owe you a bit of an explanation about what has been going on with me over the last few months. I know I have been distant and it's because I needed some space from everything that had been going on. I guess at this point we don't really owe each other anything, but I feel the need to explain myself.

Soon after we got back to New York, I was offered this new position that now has me traveling. At the time, it sounded like a great idea. Space from you may have been exactly what I needed in order for us to move on from our problems. But, with more responsibility came longer hours and less time for me to really focus on my personal life. It's not that I forgot about you – I would never be able to do that, but I became a bit overwhelmed. As you said, I had never lived in New York by myself and I too was living with strangers that I had met on Craigslist. All of our friends, outside of my work friends, were mutual friends and I hate to say it, but I felt the same way that you did when we broke up. It's like I needed to feel that way. I can't explain it, but I needed it. Your dreams had been shattered into a million tiny pieces and you couldn't help but take it out on me, even though we both knew it wasn't my fault and it made me feel like shit. I felt this time away would be a good break (even though I broke up with you, I was only intending for it to be a "break") but you were relentless in your emails and text messages that I felt suffocated. Part of me never intended for this break to be permanent, but after a while your worst fear became the truth. I wasn't in town. I was working too much. Life got in the way and I couldn't move on.

I have no ill will toward you; I just want you to know that. I know you waiver back and forth on whether or not you really hate me or are just sad from day to day, but I am not mad at you. I realize that you were going through a hard time in California and you took it out on the wrong person. I see now that you are taking the correct steps to make your life better and I am really proud of you, for whatever that's worth. Even though we haven't seen each other in months, I can tell by the tone in your emails that you are handling things well (or at least better than a few months ago). I can't image what it must have been like losing Brett, but you handled it in a very classy and mature way. Privately, I'm sure you grieved, but it seems like you've kept going to AA meetings and with this new project from your publisher, you have work and are happy. That makes me happy.

Meeting Larry was not really what I was expecting (mainly because I had just gotten out of a ten year relationship and was not looking to settle down with someone again) but he kind of swept me off my feet. As I said, he was one of Bruce's friends and we met at Claire's gallery opening. Bruce said that he thought we would be a good match and Claire agreed so we went on a date. We actually went to that Mexican place on University – that one you and I always used to go to. You know the one, with the mariachi band that comes round and sings at your table? Over margaritas, we ended up talking for hours and hitting it off really well. He's very amenable to my schedule and texts or calls me every day when I'm away. I know it's quick, but he even asked me to move in. It makes sense, since I'm never really in the city anymore. I can just keep my stuff with him and stay there on the weekends. It will be a good opportunity for us to see each other and help me financially, so I think I'm going to do it.

I know it seems quick, but I think this is the right move for me to make. Larry makes me happy and it's so easy. Things got so hard for us towards the end, that this easy-breezy relationship seems like the right choice for me. I know it's only been a few months, but there's no fighting and no screaming or name calling. I hope this doesn't hurt your feelings, but I wanted to be perfectly honest with you. I didn't want you finding out from Bruce or Claire should you end up getting in touch with them.

He's successful and I am finally finding success in my career. This seems like the right step. And look at you with your new book deal. It's like the universe is telling us that everything is going to be OK.

Best,

Gretchen

From: Gretchen Edwards
To: Max Roberts
RE: This Made Me Think of You
February 22, 2015 at 11:39 AM

Hey Max –

Haven't heard from you in a while. I hope I didn't hurt your feelings with my last email. I never want you to feel like you can't talk to me about things because, after all, you are still my best friend. I am headed to Seattle this week for five days, but will be back this weekend and have no plans if you want to get together. I would love to see you. Next week, I'm off to Vegas again but when I get back I will be moving my things into Larry's so I won't really be around. I would love to see you. Please respond and let me know if you're going to be around.

Gretchen

Text Exchange:

February 24, 2015

Gretchen to Max: I hope you don't hate me. (READ: 10:08 PM)

From: Gretchen Edwards
To: Max Roberts
RE: This Made Me Think of You
February 28, 2015 at 3:18 PM

Max —

Are you mad at me or something? I'm really sorry. I didn't mean to hurt your feelings. I am really making the choice that I think is best for me right now and I am not, in any way, trying to make you feel bad.

I know you have a lot going on right now, but it's important for me to know that you don't hate me for this. Maybe I should have told you earlier, maybe I should have run it by you, maybe I shouldn't be doing it in the first place — I don't know, but you can't ignore me forever. You are still my friend. I still care about you. Please let me know that you are OK. You haven't responded to any of my texts, calls or emails and I'm worried. I hope that this news didn't make you drink or anything. I'm really worried.

Gretchen

From: Max Roberts
To: Gretchen Edwards
RE: This Made Me Think of You
March 02, 2015, 2015 at 11:39 AM

Gretchen –

Funny, when the shoe is on the other foot how terrible it feels, huh? I went for weeks, pouring my heart out to you, with no response and the second I pull back, you can't help but to reach out. I don't know if you are trying to make yourself feel better about the questionable life choices you have made over the past few months or rub it in my face, but I find it quite a twist of fate that the moment I don't respond to you, you begin to reach out with more frequency.

I told you last month that I had to finish writing a new book and I have been working on that. I need space in order to get my thoughts and ideas together so I was really only checking work emails and calls. I wasn't trying to ignore you; I was really busy with work.

And don't flatter yourself. I didn't start drinking because you moved in with what's his name. Don't give yourself that much credit.

Max

From: Gretchen Edwards
To: Max Roberts
RE: This Made Me Think of You
March 03, 2015 at 4:44 PM

Max –

I'm sorry, I must have forgotten that you said you weren't going to be responding to emails and such. I guess I had forgotten what "off the grid" meant. I only asked if you had started drinking again because I hadn't heard from you. I know you have been through a lot over the past few months with the death of Brett, the revelation of the abortion and your living situation and such, that it was the first thing that popped in my head. You're an alcoholic. It's not an unreasonable thought.

Now that I think about it, I remember when you would go on your writing frenzies when we were living in our old apartment. I remember when you were trying to finish your first book and you were so panicked to meet your deadline that you locked yourself away in your study (which was really just a small alcove that was separated by curtains from the rest of our apartment, but you called it a study anyway). You'd listen to your music and type away furiously on your computer while I would sit on the other side of the curtain watching shitty daytime television that I had recorded. Every time you say you're writing it makes me think of our old apartment and how we lived literally on top of each other, but loved every second of it. Remember when the heat would come on in the winter and the noise sounded like a train was derailing in our apartment? There is something to be said about what you said in an email from a few weeks ago. The more I think of it, the more it's true. We really did let social media and all of that other shit consume our lives. Remember when we would sit on the sofa and try to watch our shows and all I would do is get on Instagram and see who was liking my posts? Like, what the hell is the point? No one important was trying to reach out. I probably didn't even know whoever was liking my posts personally, so what difference did it make when I could have been enjoying the person who was sitting right next to me? I'm afraid I'm as guilty of that as you are. Larry actually pointed it out. We were at the movies last weekend and I was on my phone. Like, it couldn't wait ninety minutes to check Instagram? I'm making a conscious effort to not be on my phone as much. You and Larry have both inspired me!

I hope the book is coming along nicely. What's it about, if you don't mind my asking? I was always in the know when you were writing before, it feels kind of weird not knowing what your next masterpiece will be.

Gretchen

P.S. How's the cat? I saw your Instagram photo of him a few days ago. He looked very elegant.

From: Max Roberts
To: Gretchen Edwards
RE: This Made Me Think of You
March 05, 2015 at 11:11 AM

Hey Gretchen –

Robert is very good, and yes, still very elegant, even in his old age.

You don't need to make excuses about why you're doing what you're doing. It's your life. It seems as though your conscience is guilty of something, so maybe that's something you need to work out on your end.

I've finished writing the new book, a novel, and I'm almost done with the editing process. I always have trouble with the length of things. You know me -- I like to cut to the chase. It's 2015. No one has time to create a world within their own imagination because everyone is always on the go, so I like to get my point across very clearly and very quickly, something that my publisher does not enjoy because the longer the book, the more they can charge for it.

I guess I am glad that you are happy with Larry. It seems pretty quick that you guys are cohabiting but I guess things work out the way they're supposed to or some shit like that. I must say I am kind of pissed that you said you needed space and all it really ended up with was me getting hurt again and left forever. Gretchen, if you were done for good, I really wish you would have just said that when we first broke up. I mean, I know you essentially did but you always followed it up by saying you needed time and space, leading me to believe that you intended to eventually work things out. It was very confusing. It's not really fair of you to string me along for five months only to tell me that you've not only met someone else, but now you're living with him. It seems a bit extreme. It seems as though you broke up with me for reasons other than what you initially said (I was mean, angry, et al.). Is something else going on? You can tell me.

I've stopped stalking your Instagram. I can't look at all of your pictures and follower's pictures anymore. You never blocked me, but I'm literally using the steps of AA to stop freaking out every time I see you having fun somewhere without me, and more in particular with him.

Max

From: Gretchen Edwards
To: Max Roberts
RE: This Made Me Think of You
March 06, 2015 at 1:14 PM

Max —

I am really proud of the progress that you have made in AA and how
you've come to know yourself a bit better. I think a lot of our issues in the
end were because you were a dry drunk. You never drank, but you had
the mentality of a drunk after you stopped going to meetings for so long.
It was as if you had reverted back to your drinking behavior, without ever
taking a sip of alcohol. I don't know how you even managed to not fall off
the wagon while we were in California. You seem to have gotten your life
back together and I think it's very commendable.

However, you can't take one hundred per cent of the responsibility for
what happened between the two of us. It does take two to tango. I said
that I broke up with you because I needed time to think and that is the
God's honest truth. Ten years is a long time to be with someone and I am
not the kind of person who throws the baby out with the bathwater. I was
upset with you for how you treated me in California, I really was.
However, I was really upset with myself and how I handled some of the
situations I was put in. I had aborted a baby that was yours without telling
you because I thought that it was the right thing to do. Once we got back
to New York, in a car ride that seemed to last forever and I stared at you
the entire time, not saying a word, I realized what a mistake I had made.
What I did was wrong and I was having trouble not only dealing with what
I had done, but dealing with what I had done to you. It was not my place
to make that decision alone and I felt like shit for it. You were so crushed
after our unsuccessful move to California. I know I should have told you
this earlier, but it was easier for me to say that I was mad at you for being
mean to me than to tell you truth. I guess it's too late now, since I've

moved on, but that is the truth and really what I was thinking at the time. You never gave me the space that I needed to process what I had done and it crippled me. Add on the new job and life in general, I couldn't think. I am sorry that things did not work out between us; so much happened during our relationship, more than most people go through in a lifetime, so maybe in the long run this is easier.

Life with Larry is easy. We don't fight. We get along. We live together nicely and don't argue over money. That's all I ever wanted for us and I hope – no, I know – that you will be able to find that with someone else. I just know.

I'm staying in New York this week and working at the office. If you're around and want to grab coffee, please let me know.

Gretchen

From: Max Roberts
To: Gretchen Edwards
RE: This Made Me Think of You
March 07, 2015 at 9:02 AM

Throwing the baby out with the bathwater was certainly a unique choice of words for you to make Gretchen.

We both know your side of the street is just as dirty, if not dirtier than mine. I took the brunt of the responsibility for the breakup toward the end because California was such a disaster and we were fighting all of the time, mainly because of my own insecurities and disappointment over the rejection in Cali and for the fact that I was unable to take care of you. But, it sounds like you have a few regrets of your own that are just now coming to light. I have apologized for my role in everything but as the months go on, it seems that you are having trouble coming to terms with some of your actions. Remember a few years ago when an old friend from high school contacted you and conversations got intimate and even though you said it was "never your intention for things to go there", you went there anyway? I never brought it up again. I also never did that you. I'm also relatively certain that if I had the facilities you have that I wouldn't have gone ahead and had an abortion behind your back, but that's just me.

I was taking this "break" as you called it (which just ended up ending us) to really fix my problems, the ones that you had with me and the ones that I had with myself. I've done that. Perhaps, it's time for you to look in the mirror and see what it is that has made you do some of the things that you've done. I think things seem nice with new guy and I hate to break it to you Gretchen, but every couple fights. Every couple screams. Every couple says things to each other that they don't mean. It's not rainbows and fucking sunshine every day of the year. That's not realistic and it's not real life and if you think it's going to last forever, then you are more delusional than I thought you were. The fighting leads to passion. Do you have passion with Larry or is just a picture perfect relationship on the outside? We had a bad time. The bad time ended and we moved back to New York. We got over it. Then you broke up with me once we had resolved our issues. That's not how things are supposed to go down.

I don't need your pity. I am well aware that I am completely capable of finding someone else and making them happy. And while your invitation to get together and kick it at the Regal Beagle with Larry, Janet and Jack (I've been waiting to use that, btw) I'm going to pass. I don't think you're as happy with this guy as you say you are and I have no intention of watching this charade first hand. I'm going to pass. I have a book I need to finish editing.

Max

P.S. Thank God we never had a child. You can't even be bothered to come and see the cat I got for you when I went on tour. I can only imagine I'd be left alone with a child, should we have had one.

From: Gretchen Edwards
To: Max Roberts
RE: This Made Me Think of You
March 07, 2015 at 10:18 AM

Max --

Cute "Three's Company" reference. Really funny.

I guess there really is a thin line between love and hate. You loathe me now and I suppose you have every right to. You took complete responsibility for your side of things and I really acted like a child. I'm sorry. I still do consider you a friend though, and I hope you feel the same way towards me. I know we've had a rocky road, but ten years together is nothing to scoff at. As I said, when we first broke up, I did think there was a way for us to reunite, but now there simply is not. I hope we can see each other soon. For real.

Gretchen.

P.S. Of course I miss the cat. But it's too much emotionally for me to come over to your apartment, where you are living without me, and see you guys. I think that would be too much for me to bear.

Instagram:

March 12, 2015

MaxRobertsAuthor: A Picture of a finished manuscript titled "The Story of Us." Caption: Very proud of this one!

Text Exchange:

March 17, 2015

Max to Gretchen: Happy birthday (READ: 9:14 PM)

From: Max Roberts
To: Gretchen Edwards
RE: This Made Me Think of You
April 01, 2015 at 4:15 PM

Gretchen –

I hope you are well. I'm sorry for the unpleasantness of our past few exchanges.

I figured I did not want our relationship to be for no reason. You know what I mean? That feeling of: "ugh, ten years down the drain, and for what?" I know that everyone always says that everything happens for a reason and you learn from every experience and blah, blah, blah but I finished editing my third book (as I saw you know since you liked it on Instagram) and it's called *The Story of Us* and it's literally the story of you and me. I mean, technically not you and me per se, but the story is based on us.

I know I said I would never write about you, but the more I thought about it, the more I thought of how complicated, unique, special and entertaining our relationship was and how we both ended up fucking it up. I think there is a lesson to be learned there. I turned the finished product into my publishers and they seem to love it and want it to come out later this year! I'm very happy with it and I think you will be too. I can send you a manuscript, if you'd like to read it. If not, that's OK too. I guarantee you that it's better than my last idea (the one I got stuck on – where the guy and the girl who never meet share intertwining lives and he ends up shooting her. I don't know what I was thinking with that one, but God love you for always cheering me on anyway).

I met up with Brett's parents last night, as they were in town seeing his sister who also lives here. What a terrible couple of months it has been for them. I cannot imagine dealing with the death of a child. I know I went through it privately when I dealt with the death of our unborn child, but it has got to be a totally different experience when your child has grown up, had a life, you've cared for them deeply and then they're gone. They regaled me with all of these stories from Brett's childhood and it was really lovely to take a trip down memory lane with them, even though I hadn't been there in the first place. The look on their faces every time they spoke of him was priceless. Something in their eyes really spoke to me. It's like they lit up every time his name was mentioned, but when they realized he was gone and never coming back, their expressions of happiness turned to that of sheer anguish. I feel like that's how I look when I accidentally speak about you randomly in a conversation. The second I remember that we aren't together anymore, my demeanor suddenly shifts. Sometimes I do forget you're not mine anymore.

I feel like breakups are like deaths but not as final. When someone dies, there is literally nothing you can do about it. When you break up with someone, they're still around, just not in your orbit. You have the things that make you think of them (may they be tattoos or whatever, ha!) but they're not with you anymore. Sometimes, I find myself even bringing you up in conversations, telling friends how proud I am of you for all of your accomplishments, as if we're still together. Breakups may actually be harder than a death. I know that Brett is at peace. Deep down inside this must have been what he wanted. Even if he's not at peace, there's fuck all we can do about it now. But as far as we are concerned, I am still conflicted. So many things still make me think of you but you're not here. And I don't know if I'm entirely comfortable going out with you and your new beau and pretending everything is OK. Especially when the night ends and you go home with him and not me. I'm not sure if I'm that good of an actor.

Full disclosure: I went on a date last week. With that Sandra girl (the one who Tindered me a while back). I think I told you about her at one point. She's Hungarian and I have no idea how to say her real name, but apparently when she moved here she changed it to Sandra. Isn't it weird how immigrants tend to change their names? It's as if they find a baby naming book from the 1950s, point to a name and just roll with it. I cannot tell you how many Chinese girls I have met who have the name Ester. Like six in my life. Anyway, Sandra is an artist. She's really cool and pretty. She kind of reminded me of you a bit when I first met her. She's really shy and reserved and it compliments my outrageousness and outgoingness. I told her when we sat down for dinner that it was my first date in ten and a half years and she nearly flipped. I told her that I had no idea what protocol was for a first date anymore and to be a little bit open to things that I said, as I have no idea what proper etiquette for these types of things are. Come to think of it, since we broke up, I haven't really had all that much human communication. Outside of AA, I really don't talk to many people anymore since I've stopped working at Macy's. I feel bad reaching out to our mutual friends because you are still so close with all of them and Natalie and my father only want to hear from me so much, let's be honest. So, it was nice to have a conversation with someone new and Sandra was really sweet. I think that she wanted me to go home with her, but I have zero social cues anymore, so I may also just be making that up in my head.

Anyway, just wanted to catch up. We hadn't emailed in a bit and I wanted to let you know how I was. I'm actually doing really well and hope you are as well.

Max

From: Gretchen Edwards
To: Max Roberts
RE: This Made Me Think of You
April 02, 2015 at 9:56 AM

Max –

This Sandra chick sounds lovely. I actually stalked her on Instagram and she's really, really pretty. I think she's prettier than me. So, you lucked out. I know that's a fucking obnoxious thing for me to say since I'm your ex, but it's true.

I would love to read your manuscript and am flattered that you thought that I made good enough fodder for an entire book. I saw on Instagram that it's over one hundred thousand words. I hope you were able to remain discreet about our super personal details. If there's something that bothers me in it, would you mind taking it out?

I can't believe how quickly you finished. That has got to be record time for you. I remember when you finished your first book and we had that little celebration at the Italian restaurant down on 14th Street with Bruce and Claire. We were all so proud of you and even more so when it got published.

Look at all of the wonderful things you are capable of doing. You truly are an inspiration. I'm very proud of you!

Love,

Gretchen

Text Exchange:

April 02, 2015

Gretchen: She really is pretty. (7:18 PM)
Max: I know! :) (READ: 7:49 PM)

From: Gretchen Edwards
To: Max Roberts
RE: This Made Me Think of You
April 06, 2015 at 9:02 AM

Max – I was thinking we could double date? You and Sandra and me and Larry. Don't you think that would be fun? Work is light this April and I'll be super busy in May with the new line coming out, but what do you say? Is there a night that works for you next week?

Gretchen

From: Max Roberts
To: Gretchen Edwards
RE: This Made Me Think of You
April 06, 2015 at 9:47 AM

Hey Gretchen –

I don't know if that's such a good idea. I really like Sandra and I'm trying to take it slow so I'm not sure if a double date with my ex-girlfriend and her new boyfriend is the best idea. I really appreciate you reaching out and thinking of me. Maybe you and I can grab coffee? For old time's sake? How's Tuesday?

Max

From: Gretchen Edwards
To: Max Roberts
RE: This Made Me Think of You
April 08, 2015 at 11:30 PM

Max –

We have a problem. Larry is not thrilled that we have been corresponding so frequently so I am afraid that coffee is not an option at this time. I left my email account open and I guess I had written "love" at the end of one of my messages to you and he got very mad. Larry knows a lot about our relationship (mainly because Bruce has such a big mouth) and I don't think he's very happy with us talking as much as we are and making plans. Life goes on, I guess. You will always have a very special place in my heart, Max. I hope you know that.

Gretchen

From: Max Roberts
To: Gretchen Edwards
RE: This Made Me Think of You
April 09, 2015 at 10:07 AM

Gretchen –

I have to say I am very disappointed that Larry thought it was inappropriate that we were communicating. I think it's inappropriate to snoop on your girlfriend's laptop, but I guess that's just me. No offense to him, but dude just like popped into the picture a few months ago. We have ten years of history and memories together. You can't just cut me off at the knees like that. I thought that we were moving forward and maybe trying to have a friendship or something, but I guess not.

I don't think I care for Larry very much.

Max

Venmo:

April 1, 2015: Gretchen to Larry W.: "Rent"
April 2, 2015: Larry W. to Gretchen: "Take your rent back ;)"
April 19, 2015: Gretchen to Claire: "Draaaaaaaaaanks!"

From: Max Roberts
To: Gretchen Edwards
RE: This Made Me Think of You
April 19, 2015 at 2:39 PM

Gretchen –

I had the strangest dream last night and you were in it. We were standing above the entrance to the 18th Street subway line (you know – on the 1 line. That random station that's like two blocks from two other stations but still exists for some reason. That never made sense to me). Anyway, we were standing there and you whispered to me "hurry, we have to catch the train". But the train wasn't coming. You were wearing that slinky black dress that you wore to my second book launch but I was wearing oversized, shabby clothes that were nearly threadbare. You grabbed my hand and pulled me down the subway entrance so fast that it seemed almost like we were gliding down the stairs, our feet never touching the floor. Once we got to the platform, the train suddenly arrived and you grabbed my hand to follow you onto the car, but I pulled away and walked onto a different car – a car with no one on it. I turned around to see you in the car behind me and Larry mysteriously appeared, dressed in a tuxedo. I suppose my subconscious knew what he looked like from your Instagram account. The two of you looked very much in love and suddenly the car that I was on pulled away from yours and the two of you just got smaller and smaller in the distance. Then I woke up. I'm not exactly sure what this all means, but it was really odd.

Things are moving along nicely with the editing of the book. My publishers really like it and think it's going to be a huge success. As soon as it's copyedited, I will send it your way.

I'm still talking to Sandra. She's a really nice girl and gorgeous to boot. We haven't been intimate because I'm still a little nervous to do that with anyone else. I know it probably doesn't make any sense, but it still just doesn't feel right. I can't put my finger on it – maybe it's just the fact that we had such a good rhythm in the bedroom; I don't want to try with someone else because it might not live up to what we had. I know, it's stupid, but it's how I feel. I would never tell Sandra that, because I am sure she would be devastated, but it's the truth.

Sometimes when I am lonely, I will go on Tinder and talk to other girls. You know, just for fun. Sandra and I aren't exclusive so I don't really feel bad about it. It's so weird what people are looking for on there. So many girls just want someone to cuddle with. Call me old fashioned, but don't you think you should do that with someone you love or at least went out for drinks with beforehand? I guess I've never been the kind of guy to sleep with girls or cuddle with them before getting to know them. I guess it's because we were together for so long, I don't really know how to be single.

To be honest with you Gretchen, if you asked me to take you back right now, I would. Not because it's comfortable and not because I miss you but because this time apart has really made me realize just how much I fucking love you. Sorry, I shouldn't have said that but it's true.

Max

From: Max Roberts
To: Gretchen Edwards
RE: This Made Me Think of You
May 01, 2015 at 7:58 PM

Gretchen –

Hi! I hope you are doing well. I haven't heard from you in a while so I wanted to drop a line and see what was going on. Has the Max embargo been lifted yet or is Larry still content on us not talking? It's really fucking weird not hearing from you for long periods of time.

Things with Sandra are moving along nicely, but I must say it's a very different situation from ours. She's from another country, so it's nice to find out about her culture and see how different her upbringing was than mine. I guess it wasn't entirely that different, I basically grew up in the ghettos of Baltimore and she grew up in the ghettos of Budapest. Same story, different locale I suppose. She's really nice and she takes me to all of these weird places in the East Village that look like you're either going to get Asbestos poisoning or e-Coli from upon entering, but it's fun to explore new things. It's definitely stuff we would never do together and I am not sure if that's a good thing or a bad thing. It's just a different thing, I suppose.

Some of my AA buddies have congratulated me for moving on with someone new, but I'm not completely happy about it. I felt that you and I had the best relationship two people could ever have and that anything else will always be second best. Maybe that's just how I view it. It's kind of like going to see the best Broadway show you've ever seen on their opening night. The show is flawless, the most exciting and spectacular you've ever seen. Then, you go back a few years later to see it again, with the memory of how wonderful it was the first time around. The show is the same, but the energy is lower. The costumes are worse for the wear, the sets don't shine as much as they did before, some of the cast members hearts just aren't in it anymore and it shows. When you leave the show, you realize you've tried to recreate an amazing experience that will simply never be the same again. That's how I feel with Sandra.

I'm thinking of taking another room somewhere else. I'm still not completely comfortable where I am now and since I have a bit more money than I did a few months ago, I think it may be time for me to move on. Again, I don't have my own furniture here and the people I live with have offered to get rid of it for me so that I can get new stuff, but something about this place just doesn't feel right. So many bad things have happened here. You broke up with me, Brett died, I was on a shame spiral for several months and the cat keeps pooping on the floor instead of his poop box for some reason. It's bad karma or something. I want to get out of here.

I went to check out how things were going for you via Instagram and it seems as though you have either blocked me or are no longer on it. When my computer broke, I unfortunately lost all of the pictures I had of us so now I really don't have many memories or you and me. When I saw that you had deleted all of the pictures of us that you had on Instagram, I did the same and now I don't have much left. I have a wallet sized picture of us that I keep on me at all times, but I haven't taken it out much lately because I don't want Sandra to see it.

She's really good about dealing with my memories and stuff of you, but I don't want to shove it in her face. I told her everything that happened and she told me that she thought that we had been through so much in the past year and that it's more than most couples have to deal with for their entire lives. It really is true. Sometimes, I cry in the middle of the night, missing you. I lie to her and tell her that I am sad about Brett, and maybe I am sometimes. I hate lying to her, but it's true. Not a day has gone by in the past nine months that I haven't thought of you. But I am doing everything humanly possible to move on. I guess these things just take longer than you expect.

Max

Twitter:

May 03, 2015

@maxrobertsauthor: That moment when you finally start getting over your ex and TimeHop reminds you of something fun you did on this day three years ago.

From: Max Roberts
To: Gretchen Edwards
RE: This Made Me Think of You
May 05, 2015 at 9:17 PM

Gretchen –

Breakups are so fucking weird. I wish there was a class they taught in college that helped you navigate your way through experiences like this. It's like never ending. Do you ever get over someone you loved with your entire heart? We have gone from yelling and screaming to pointing fingers to taking space to basically not talking anymore. When we first broke up, I began reading all of these silly books on "how to get your ex back". All any of them ever said was that you need to trick your ex back into loving you again. I don't know why I even bothered spending the money, as they clearly didn't work. Ha!

Would you have ever thought two years ago that we would be where we are now? Living separately and dating other people? I really thought we would be together forever and I know you did as well. Two years ago, we had it made and we didn't even know it. Two years ago, we were comfortable and sometimes being comfortable is better than whiling away the days wondering what could have been, or even worse, acting on those feelings. Comfortable is good and it can be happy. We had our little routine and it was nice. We'd meet at home for dinner almost every night after work, watch our shows, make love (depending on the day and the time of the month), go to sleep and do it again the next day. On the weekends we would see our friends and go out. It was actually kind of perfect, when you think about it.

Why the fuck did we move to California?

It ruined everything. We had such big dreams. We saw our comfortability as settling and instead of enjoying what we had, we made up something up in our minds of what life could be and that became what kept us going. We made a plan to conquer our dreams and when it quickly turned into a nightmare, we scattered. We stopped taking care of each other the way we had before and I believe with my whole heart that that was our downfall. God I wish there was a time machine and I could go back to two years ago and say to myself: *dude, you have it made, chill.* I took you for granted because I never thought you'd leave me. If only I hadn't.

Breakups are fucking weird. I'm sorry that we are still going through it and that your space led you to someone who you feel will take better care of you. I feel like less of a man without you. You are my heart and soul. I hate to say it, but I would kick Sandra to the curb for just one more night with you.

Max

Facebook:

May 08, 2015 at 6:10 PM

Gretchen Edwards is engaged to Larry Wolek.

From: Max Roberts
To: Gretchen Edwards
RE: This Made Me Think of You
May 08, 2015 at 2:47 PM

Gretchen –

Wow. You're engaged? I couldn't even get a heads up? What the fuck
Gretchen?

From: Gretchen Edwards
To: Max Roberts
RE: This Made Me Think of You
May 08, 2015 at 5:38 PM

Max —

I'm so sorry that you had to find out about our engagement via Facebook. That is not what I had intended to happen. I was going to call you today to tell you over the phone, because at the end of the day, you really deserve that and so much more. I know we are broken up, but you know I still care about you.

Listen, Larry and I have really hit it off and love living together. We don't have any of the issues that you and I had — we rarely fight, we don't argue over money, we just have a great time together. I know it seems fast, but I love him and I feel in my heart that this is the right choice for me to make. I'm over thirty and I want to start a family and Larry does too. We are both at points in our careers where it makes sense to take the next step. I'm happy, I really am and I hope that you can understand that. There are none of the issues we had — there's no unattainable dream we're focused on, what we have is real and tangible and right.

I'm really happy right now, Max and I hope that you can be happy as well. I know that I'm asking a lot, but if you really do still love me, you will understand that this is what I want. I don't want what we had anymore, I want this.

I really do hope that we can all meet up at some point soon and you can get a chance to meet him. I really think you'd like Larry.

Take care, Gretchen

From: Max Roberts
To: Gretchen Edwards
RE: This Made Me Think of You
May 10, 2015 at 7:18 AM

Gretchen –

I guess I just don't understand what happened. Our "break" led to your engagement to someone else. You said you were taking all of this time to try to find yourself and it just led you to him.

Listen, I will leave you alone once and for all. I don't think I can mentally take much more of this back and forth anyway. Last night after I found out about your pending nuptials, I found this letter in an old jacket pocket that I wrote you a few years ago after we had had a spat. It made me think of you, and how much I love you.

I just want to tell you how deeply I love you. I remember when we first met and how I didn't want to get into a relationship with you because the odds were stacked against us but I relented. And I'm so happy that I did.

You've taught me how to love -- how to really love and how to give myself to someone else. You taught me how to love myself more. I've never felt this way about someone before and maybe that's why I'm so sorry we got into a fight. You are my breath, my air, my water, you are what makes me live.

I never truly understood what people meant when they referred to their spouses or boyfriends or girlfriends as their "other half" until I met you. You truly are my other half, another part of me that I didn't realize I was missing until you came along. You are my world, my everything, my special girl. My second self.

I wrote this letter in hopes that you'll remember how much I love you and forget that we had gotten into this fight. I was having a bad day and shouldn't have started a pointless fight.

Take your time and hopefully you will be able to stop being so mad. Time heals everything. But time will never heal my undying love for you.

I am always on your side. I am always here for you. I will never forget you and I will love you forever. You are my heart, my lungs, my eyes, my everything. I am ready to come back when you're ready to have me.

I will love you until the day I die and every day after that.

Max

Go back and count how many times you said "I'm really happy now" in your last email. Who are you trying to prove it to? Happy people don't need to tell everyone how frigging happy they are, they're just happy.

Best of luck with everything,

Max

From: Gretchen Edwards
To: Max Roberts
RE: This Made Me Think of You
May 29, 2015 at 7:19 PM

Max –

I hope you are having a wonderful Memorial Day weekend. I saw on Instagram (I blocked you but can still see what you're doing) that you guys went up to Boston for the weekend. That must have been fun. It made me think of that time that we went to Boston to see your sister when she was at BU. Remember how much fun we had that weekend? I certainly hope that you are having that much fun with Sandra.

I just wanted to let you know that I have a box of your stuff at my place. I did a full clear out of my storage unit (finally) and there were a few things that you left behind from when you got your stuff a few months ago as well as some furniture that you had brought up from Baltimore when we originally moved here. Jesus, our shit was all over the place for so long, it's nice to know that everything is where it needs to be.

Let me know if you would like to come and pick it up or if you'd like to pop by my office. I suppose I could mail it as well. Is your address still the same?

Let me know what you'd like to do about all of this.

Gretchen

Text Exchange:

May 30, 2015

Max: Got your email. I have no idea what I could have possibly left in storage. Not important. You can throw it out. (1:13 PM)
Gretchen: OK. (READ: 2:23 PM)

From: Gretchen Edwards
To: Max Roberts
RE: This Made Me Think of You
June 09, 2015 at 8:23 PM

Max –

I feel like I've upset you and that was never my intention. I know that things didn't work out the way that we had originally planned (when do they ever?) but can we at least open up a dialogue and try to talk about this?

Just because I am marrying someone else doesn't mean that I don't still care about you. I will always care about you no matter what. Please let me know that you are OK.

Gretchen

From: Gretchen Edwards
To: Max Roberts
RE: This Made Me Think of You
June 14, 2015 at 8:30 PM

Max –

Still nothing. Please get in touch so we can chat. We haven't spoken on the phone since we broke up in September, I would love to at least hear your voice.

From: Gretchen Edwards
To: Max Roberts
RE: This Made Me Think of You
June 19, 2015 at 4:21 PM

Max –

Please pick up the phone when I call. I need to talk to you.

Gretchen

From: Max Roberts
To: Gretchen Edwards
RE: This Made Me Think of You
June 20, 2015 at 3:01 PM

Gretchen –

I have no idea what you could possibly want to talk about at this point. I mean, Jesus Christ, you're fucking engaged. I understand that I am no longer in your life and I accept it. I'm not happy about it, but I accept it. It is what it is.

Eleven years ago, I was walking in the university parking lot and there stood a girl, with silky blond hair, crying hysterically because she thought someone had stolen her rental car. You were nineteen, almost twenty, an absolute bombshell and so naïve. When we finally figured out that your rental car had not, in fact, been stolen and you had just forgotten not only where you had parked it, but what it looked like, you jumped for joy into my arms and laid a kiss on me. Then we made out in the back of said rental car for hours. Little did I know that from that moment on, you would be my world, my universe. It's so funny how life works out. If you hadn't crashed your car, had your parents get you a rental in the meantime and then subsequently "lost" said rental we would have never met and my life would be completely different. You helped me to follow my dreams and led me straight to New York where we spent eight wonderful years together. Then, we moved to California and everything changed. Now, we're strangers. It's insane how life can change so quickly. How the cast of characters that populate our everyday affairs are fleeting, even when you think they'll be with you forever. How, if I had stayed and studied in the library the night that I had met you (like I was supposed to) and not left early, I would have never seen you crying in the parking lot. Imagine what our lives would be if we had never met.

I don't really need to speak to you because I am not entirely sure you have anything new to say to me that I haven't already heard. I am allowed to feel that way. I'm sorry, I assumed that you were taking this break in order to try and work things out with me. Why else would you insist on taking a break? Because if your original plan was to simply leave me then saying you need a break and space after our breakup was wrong. Funny, all of these ways to communicate and we still misinterpret everything we say to each other. Regardless of whether or not I wrote or texted you during said break, we never spoke to each other over the phone nor did we ever see each other in person. You had ample time to figure your shit out and you did – just not with me.

I don't have much left to say to you Gretchen. My feelings are deeply hurt and I don't want to get into this over the phone or in person.

Best of luck with Larry.

Max

From: Gretchen Edwards
To: Max Roberts
RE: This Made Me Think of You
June 21, 2015 at 11:46 AM

Max –

You have to pick up the phone when I call you. I am truly sorry that you feel this way, I really am, but I have moved on. It doesn't mean that I don't care about you or love you – I will always love you as a person but my heart is with Larry now.

I hope you understand. I wish you would pick up the phone when I call you.

Gretchen

From: Max Roberts
To: Gretchen Edwards
RE: This Made Me Think of You
June 22, 2015 at 1:13 PM

Gretchen –

I really don't owe you a phone call or anything at all.

A few weeks ago, Sandra and I spent the weekend in Atlantic City. Remember our trips down there? We'd go down for the weekend, turn off our phones and spend the days just staring at the ocean like two old people who had nothing better to do with their lives. We always found something about looking out onto the sea so calming, and of course our never ending love of old things that used to be nice that aren't anymore. What's the word again? Sandra did not seem to have the same affinity for AC that you have. She thought it was dirty and ghetto and unseemly. I tried to explain to her what it was about the place that I loved so much but something got lost in translation. Sandra and I did all of the things that you and I used to do and love. We strolled on the boardwalk, we ate buffet (I had a coupon so you know I was very excited to use it) and we sat in front of a slot machine (an American pastime that apparently she didn't appreciate as much as I do). But something was wrong. She wasn't you. No one will ever be you. She didn't even nag me for spending too much money like you always used to do. She didn't care. She clearly didn't want to be there at all.

I suppose it's either my alcoholism talking or my lack of being able to let things go or both, but this past year has emotionally crippled me. Coming back from California defeated, only to lose you, finding a new friend in Brett only to lose him, and the general feeling of being lost in the middle of an emotional sea of shit without a paddle has left me completely numb. I now think I am immune to any emotion whatsoever. I'm never especially happy, sad or depressed. The only reason I got even the slightest bit of excited when I finished my last book was because I thought that it was going to impress you, which it did not. I stopped working at the website I was writing for because it did nothing for me. People click the links on my Facebook profile – big fucking deal. It brought me no joy. I've seemed to have lost whatever spark it was that kept me going. I am on autopilot twenty-four hours of the day, seven days a week. I feel completely empty.

I thought that having Sandra around was going to make me happier because everyone always says, "move on, you'll find someone new" and "someone else will make you just as happy as Gretchen did". And I did, but she didn't. She's wonderful. She is, in fact, perfect. She is caring, sweet, drop dead beautiful and always there for me. Sandra and I never fight like you and I used to. The only thing she isn't is you. She used to make me think of you every time I would see her but now when I look at her, all I can think about is how she isn't you. Her hair is shorter than yours. She doesn't have that funny little birthmark thing on her lip or ugly tree tattoo on her back. She doesn't laugh at all of my ridiculously stupid jokes that only you find funny. Anyone from the outside looking in would have simply thought that I had traded you in for a newer, more exotic model. But she isn't you and never will be.

The other thing that has haunted me for the past few months is this unquenchable thirst for booze. When I texted you that night a few months back and told you that I may drink, I was only telling the half-truth. I was fishing when I texted you that night, not so much because I wanted to drink, but because I wanted to let you know how hurt I was – which was childish and immature. I don't know what I thought I was going to accomplish by telling you that I was considering drinking but I guess I wanted to make you feel bad. I wanted you to know how hurt I was by everything that happened and that I just couldn't take it. You don't know what it's like to think that the person you love most in the world hates you more than anyone else in the world. I made you miserable, and yes, you certainly hurt my feelings too but you wouldn't have done what you did unless I had driven you to the point of wanting to have an abortion behind my back. You don't know what it's like to know that you have caused someone you love that much pain. It's unbearable to live with.

I bent over backwards to try and win you back. The tattoo, me telling you that I had a ring, and of course apologizing and taking responsibility for everything that I had done. That takes a lot. To list off the things that you have done wrong, take responsibility for them and make a conscious effort not to do them ever again is one of the hardest things that we as humans can do. I humbled myself to the point of humiliation and I told you that, given the chance, I would never make the same mistakes again. I know I've gotten pissed at you since then, but can you honestly blame me? You were too hurt to let me back in. Perhaps that's my fault. Or perhaps you find some sick pleasure in relishing in the bad memories of our past. You've held on to how I treated you for so long. I know you need to do that in order to be at peace with the decisions you've made. You've pushed out the good and focus only on the bad so that you can be comfortable moving on from me. Why have you done that? Has it made you any happier? Has it helped you move on with Larry? We're done now and since you won't give me another chance, what exactly has holding on to these bad memories given you?

A few weeks ago when Sandra and I went to Atlantic City and I could see that she was not having any of it, I thought to myself, *what the fuck is the point of this?* What is the point of trying if it's all going to go to hell? Sure, everything happens for a reason and you learn a life lesson from everything and blah, blah, blah. Sandra encourages me to try to be with her and she is very sweet, but if things don't work out then I don't know if I have the mental bandwidth to go through what I am going through with you all over again with her. But I've been through it. I never let go of losing my mother. I never let go of losing you and I never let go of losing

Brett. Why stay sober if I am just going to be miserable all of the time? A few weeks ago I was going to AA meetings seven to ten times a week, therapy and working out every day. Maybe I am one of the lost souls who never manages to find their way to a happy sober life, like the ones you read about in the literature; the unfortunates they always speak of at the beginning of meetings. Maybe I'm emotionally disabled and incapable of leading a healthy, happy sober life. So, when Sandra gave up on trying to like Atlantic City and went to the room to go to sleep without me, I stayed out and stood on The Boardwalk and looked out onto the ocean. This was the exact picturesque backdrop that I had hoped to propose to you under, but you weren't there. I stood stationary for several hours, watching the waves crash into the shore, momentarily turning my attention to the strollers along The Boardwalk. Everyone looked so happy and here I was, poor pathetic Max. I felt abandoned and alone. Everyone had left me, including Sandra who was now up in the hotel room, and I was alone.

I really may never know why it's impossible for me to get over you. Maybe it's the fact that even though I am thirty years old, this is my first breakup. Maybe it's because you seem to be making an effortless transition into a new life with Larry and I can't move on at all. Maybe it's because I held out too much hope. Maybe it's because you only get one great love of life and you're mine but I am not yours. I don't understand the point of giving yourself fully to another human being only to have it taken away. It's an emptiness I've never experienced in my life and it kind of seems pointless in the end. Whatever the reason is, after standing on The Boardwalk like a confused old man who had wandered from the nursing home, I walked back into the casino, sat at the bar, ordered a whisky and drank. And I didn't just drink one, oh no, I drank many. It's exactly what people in the program who have left the program and come back in said it would be. It didn't make me feel much better and I could not stop. I not only drank for hours but I also drained my bank account of any liquid funds I had because I decided to gamble all of my money away. I gambled and drank my entire book advance away. I was a mess, but I wasn't home, so at the casino I was just another random drunk guy who had a little too much fun. I went back up to my room in the middle of the night to find Sandra sleeping peacefully without a care in the world.

I don't know what it is that I don't get about life. How some things happen and there is no rhyme or reason to it. Why do people have to die? What the fuck is the point of living if we are all just going to die? Why do we get into relationships if they're all inevitably going to end? I haven't learned much from our breakup. I thought I had learned to use my AA pathos in life a little better, but considering I just fell off the wagon, I suppose that's shot to shit now too. I cannot move on. I've given it time and it's not working. I haven't drank a drop of alcohol since Atlantic City and I haven't even told anyone what happened, including Sandra, until now.

If we had stayed in New York and not moved to California, our lives would be so much better. They would be better because we would be together and you know that for a fact. Now, you're engaged to someone else and I am just, once again, turned into the fall down drunk you felt bad for in college.

Max

From: Gretchen Edwards
To: Max Roberts
RE: This Made Me Think of You
June 23, 2015 at 9:16 AM

Oh, Max. Why didn't you call me?

If you were feeling like you were going to drink, you could have picked up the phone to call and I of course would have answered. I really hope that you haven't had a drink since. I know firsthand how important your sobriety was to you and I feel horrible that you felt so hopeless and alone. I guess a lot of that is my fault.

I do not think you are a villain, by any means. We had a rough time and you overreacted to a lot of things that happened in California. I was fortunate enough to have a job, but the pace there and the fact that it was such a different way of life threw you for a complete loop. It wasn't just in California though. If you'll remember, we had fought before we even moved there. Granted, it wasn't as bad as after we moved across the country but it was still bad. Yes, you made me feel great and at times you made me feel better than anyone else ever had before in my life. But when you made me feel bad, you made me feel like the worst person in the world and that is something that I have had a hard time getting over. I understand that all relationships have their road blocks and life isn't always fun but you took it to the extreme. How many times was I going to have to forgive you for lashing out at me? There's only so much a girl can take.

I'm not mad at you anymore. I have moved on. I don't want you to think that I hate you, because it's quite the opposite. I love you. I might not love you as a boyfriend anymore, but I certainly still love you as a person. I wouldn't be where I am today without you and for that I will forever be grateful. Seriously, I will. I don't know if I would have ever had the courage to move to New York and pursue a career in fashion without you. I certainly wouldn't have made it through school without you. And I wouldn't know how to love someone else with my whole entire heart if I had never met you. I am truly happy to know you but I don't want you to waste away your sobriety over me. I mean, I know you already drank but I really hope that you find yourself back in the program. What happened to your sponsor? And what happened to that Chuck guy? I thought you two were getting friendly?

Please take care of yourself, Max. I don't want you to drink and I don't want you to feel this way. You have to try and move on. Not for me, but for yourself.

Gretchen

From: Max Roberts
To: Gretchen Edwards
RE: This Made Me Think of You
June 25, 2015 at 6:14 PM

Gretchen –

Thank you for the kind words.

I really have jumped head first back into the program. I told the few
friends I have there what happened and they were so kind and
understanding to me. I was very ashamed of what I had done. I didn't
drink because I necessarily wanted to drink. I drank because I felt alone,
abandoned and lost. What's weird though is going back to AA and
listening to everyone talk about how much they either liked drinking or
want to drink. It's a lot of talking about drinking, which kind of makes me
want to drink.

I have also been in therapy a bit, which was helped (a little). Talking to
people about my problems has never really made me feel much better, it
only reminds me that I have problems and now we're talking about them.
My therapist says that I have deep rooted abandonment issues that stem
from my mother's death, you leaving and Brett killing himself. I could
have told you that for free but this maniac charges like $175 an hour for
it. I know I have abandonment issues. I never wanted to get left behind as
a child and I still don't today but continuously am.

What I have trouble dealing with is the fact that you can give and give and
give to someone and it doesn't seem to matter at all. Have you ever
thought about that? We as human beings are told that we need to pair
off, to mate and make babies, and in doing that we express a certain level
of desire for one another that separates us from the animals. But then
what happens when it's all over? Do you get those things back? I'm not
talking about money or property or anything like that. I'm talking about

those late night chats, expressing your feelings, helping someone else out at your own expense. What happens to those things? Allegedly, they come back to you from another person, but I don't really buy that shit. For example, Sandra is very open and kind to all of my issues, but I really couldn't care less (don't tell her that if you ever meet her). I want it back from you and I will never get it. It's very troubling to me.

I think Sandra is going to be done with me soon. We have been dating all this time and we still haven't had sex yet. I know, crazy, right? I just can't bring myself to do it. She's so attractive and everything a man could want in a woman but we still have not done the deed. I am not sure what's holding me back, but I think part of it is if we do make love then you and I will officially be over, and for some reason I am holding on for dear life that we aren't. I know it's fucked up but true. I don't even know why I am trying so hard with her, not that I really am. I guess she's just another distraction to pass the time.

I'm sorry to bother you with all of this. I am literally back at Step One in AA and trying to once again give my will up to God (whoever the hell he is) and try to get my life back on track.

Hope you are having a great day!

Max

Text Exchange:

June 26, 2015

Gretchen: Remember that gross little diner that we used to eat at all the time on 52nd? (5:45 PM)
Max: Yeah. (6:08 PM)
Gretchen: Larry hates it. (6:11 PM)
Max: Eh. (READ: 6:13 PM)

From: Gretchen Edwards
To: Max Roberts
RE: This Made Me Think of You
July 01, 2015 at 4:14 PM

Max –

There are a lot of things that Larry does that make me think of you and a lot of things that Larry doesn't do that make me wish he were you.

I know I shouldn't be saying this, but he's not as much fun as you are. Remember how we would go to Coney or Atlantic City and just revel in the trash? Maybe it's because we are trash, lol. Larry is so fancy and insists on going to expensive dinners out almost every night. Sure, at first it was awesome. I was like, "Max, the writer who makes no money, could never afford places like this," but after a while it got so boring. He doesn't make me laugh like you do either. Remember that time we were walking down the street and those two older women from Pennsylvania needed directions? You showed them exactly where to go, walked them to the door of the restaurant they were looking for and then we proceeded to eat a four hour meal with them and found out that one of them was actually friends with your Aunt Ruth? Larry barely acknowledges his doorman so nothing like that would ever happen with him. You have a zest for life that not too many people do. So when I heard that you had fallen off the wagon it really affected me. I felt bad, but I also didn't want you feeling the sadness you must have felt before you took that drink. I know how hard you have worked and so it must have been bad.

Larry and I have been bickering over wedding arrangements and it's been a pain in the ass. Remember how we used to argue over stupid shit like the color of our curtains? Well, imagine that times a million. I guess Larry and I don't really know each other as well as we thought because we can't seem to agree on much these days. Claire told me that this is how every couple acts when they are planning a wedding and that it brings a level of stress to a relationship that many people don't understand until they're going through it. Well, I'm going through it now and I don't like it. I thought this was supposed to be fun – a celebration of our love for each other, but every time we talk about it (and he gets his mother involved who always has to throw her two cents into the ring) I feel like I'm in the Thunderdome.

I'm sure this will pass. I really hope you are feeling better.

Gretchen

P.S. You and Sandra really haven't had sex yet?

From: Max Roberts
To: Gretchen Edwards
RE: This Made Me Think of You
July 02, 2015 at 3:13 PM

No, Sandra and I have not had sex, a fun fact that she likes to bring up every time she's in the mood. I told her I wasn't ready and she tells me that I am acting like a teenage girl who's about to get her cherry popped. I even suggested waiting until marriage, but she was certainly not up for that. She's also allergic to cats so I can't have her over to my place and she has about seven Russian roommates and lives in Brooklyn; all of the above just seem like too much work for me.

As far as the Larry stuff goes, Gretchen, I don't really know if it's my place to comment on all of that. But, as I told you before, and as you refused to listen, every couple fights. It just fucking happens, unfortunately. All I can say is that if you have any doubt about any of this, maybe jumping into a marriage isn't the best thing for you. I don't know from experience, but I can only imagine that planning a wedding is a huge deal and not to be taken lightly. Also, deciding to get married and sharing your life and finances and all of that other bullshit with someone else is a huge deal too. It's not something to jump into if you're not ready, so I would say if you're having doubts, maybe take a step back and look at what's really going on. Are you using Larry as a mechanism for moving on from me or do you really love and want to marry him?

I would really think about it. You haven't been with him for that long. You all can't possibly know each other that well. Take a step back and look at the big picture. Max

From: Gretchen Edwards
To: Max Roberts
RE: This Made Me Think of You
July 03, 2015 at 10:49 PM

Max –

I appreciate your thoughts and really think you should sleep with Sandra even if she lives in Brooklyn. Come on!

What's weird is how everyone around me tells me that Larry and I are the perfect fit, but for some reason I keep feeling that there is a piece missing. I don't know if it's because I got so used to you and how you do things or not, but it's different. He's not as open as you are. I guess it's because you're a creative and he's more business oriented but he just doesn't have that thing you do. I can't put my finger on it. I don't know if anyone else ever will and I can't really explain it, but it's like I'm constantly looking for something that doesn't exist. I've tried, but it's just not there.

I am going to go through with the wedding though because something deep down inside of me tells me that it is the right thing to do. While Larry doesn't have some of the qualities that you possess, he does have stability (which you never had), he never yells at me (which you did quite a bit, but we do bicker), and he is classy (not that you aren't but I guess he can afford to be classier). I guess those were the things that were missing from our relationship that I thought I really needed and have found in him. No one is ever going to be perfect, but he does fit a lot of the criteria I am looking for and I am happy with him, despite the few things he is missing.

Our wedding is set for next year. We decided to have a long engagement. I really hope that we are on good enough terms by then that you will make it. I really want you there and Larry will just have to deal with it –G

From: Max Roberts

To: Gretchen Edwards
RE: This Made Me Think of You
July 03, 2015 at 11:56 PM

Gretchen –

Yeah, we will see how the whole "me attending the wedding" thing plays out. I don't know if I will ever be ready to watch you marry another man, but we'll see.

As far as finding your "perfect man", I suppose I am happy for you. I'm trying to turn over a new leaf and not be the ex who begs you to come back over and over again. I think that had a lot to do with my relapse and I don't want to go back to that place. I do still obviously love and care about you and I am pretty sure that you know that. I also realize that at this point, you aren't coming back. If you were going to change your mind, you would have done so a while back. Considering the fact that you are about to marry someone else, I would say it's safe to say this is over.

Having said that, part of me really doesn't feel like you're one hundred per cent invested in this. You keep pointing out his shortcomings instead of the things that you really like (I'm actually not even sure what it is that you like about him) and it's troublesome. I really hope that you have thought long and hard about this decision. If you are having reservations, then you should really think about what's going on. I don't want to see you end up hurt in the long run. You haven't known each other for that long and you've made several huge life choices regarding him over the past few months. It is a little fast. I know we aren't getting any younger but come on.

I finally had sex with Sandra. It was really awkward. Mainly because she basically threw herself at me. I know that we have been dating for a quite some time and it seems ridiculous to have not had sex yet, but I still wasn't ready and I am pretty sure that she knew it. It was kind of nice though. You know, to have human contact. I used to fantasize about the last time we made love and that would get me through the day. Honestly, I kind of did that when I was with Sandra. I know it's wrong, but it's true. At least I got it over with.

Max

From: Gretchen Edwards
To: Max Roberts
RE: This Made Me Think of You
July 04, 2015 at 12:31 PM

Max –

I know that coming from me this doesn't mean much, but if you don't have real feelings for Sandra maybe it's best that you move on. I know that probably sounds crazy coming from me, the girl who is engaged to someone she's known for only a few months, but I honestly do feel that. Life is too short to hold to things that don't mean a lot to you. It's a waste of time. On the flip side, perhaps it was good that you got a little sex under your belt. You probably needed it. Who am I to tell you what you need, though? Anyway, best of luck with everything. I'm sure we will speak soon!

Gretchen

From: Max Roberts
To: Gretchen Edwards
RE: This Made Me Think of You
July 29, 2015 at 7:19 PM

Gretchen –

Well I have some rather surprising news that even shocked me.

I'm moving to London!

Isn't that crazy? A book publishing company was really interested in hiring me for a full time editing position there and after a few online interviews that I did on a whim, thinking I'd never get it, I found out today that they hired me! I'm so excited. They are paying for my move and everything and the money is great. I know, I have a new book coming out in a few months, but this is a great opportunity for me and I am really looking forward to pursuing it. You know how hard it is to get an editing gig at a publishing company and the offer is too good to refuse.

Unfortunately, Sandra was not interested in either moving to London or having a long distance relationship so we have parted ways. I kind of saw it coming. She was so great in dealing with everything regarding my feelings toward you and our breakup, but I think we both knew that it was never meant to be. She has a huge art installation opening here in a few months that she's super excited about and didn't think it was appropriate to move to London or focus her energy on a guy who was living an ocean away. I whole heartedly understand her position and I have to say it's kind of a relief. Keeping up appearances with her and pretending that I wasn't over you was becoming draining. I liked her but it just wasn't a fit.

Anyway, I leave in a month. I know you are probably busy and won't have a chance to see me before I go. I will also be super busy wrapping up working on the book and need to make sure that everything is taken care of before I head out of town, so I just wanted to check in and tell you that I am hopping across the pond indefinitely. I'm taking Robert down to Baltimore to live with Natalie. Unfortunately, I can't take him with me to another country. I love him to death, but seeing the cat really makes me think of you and I think I really need to take this opportunity as a true fresh start. I know Natalie will take great care of him, so I am not worried about it.

Maybe our breakup was good for me, after all. I would have never had even considered applying for a job in London if we were still together. All I ever wanted was California and look at where it's taken me!

Max

Venmo Payments July 29:
London Prime Publishing to Max: "Payment for Move"
Max to Natalie R.: "Money for Robert. Take care of my baby! Thanks!"
Max to Sandra B.: "For that shirt I ruined. Sorry. Take care."

From: Gretchen Edwards
To: Max Roberts
RE: This Made Me Think of You
July 30, 2015 at 4:09 PM

Max –

Congratulations on your new position. I am very excited for you. Sad that things didn't work out with Sandra, but I guess that's to be expected considering the emotional state you've been in over the year. Wow, it's almost been a year since we've been together. Can you believe that? It's like so much has happened, but nothing has happened at all. It's hard to explain, but I still feel so close to you even though we haven't seen each other or spoken over the phone in so long. The world we live in! I have to say that I am a little sad that you are leaving town and we won't have a chance to see each other again anytime soon. You are right and I am totally swamped with traveling for work. I know you will be insane trying to get your things settled here in order to leave, finish your book, packing, etc. Speaking of which, you never sent me a copy of your new book and you said you would. Will you please pop it in the mail before you go? I would really love to read it. Kiss Robert for me! I miss him every day!

I'm so proud of you, Max.

Gretchen

From: Max Roberts
To: Gretchen Edwards
RE: This Made Me Think of You
August 30, 2015 at 6:08 AM

Gretchen –

I'm sorry I have been out of touch. I leave for London in the morning and I have been busy trying to put the pieces of my new life together, brick by brick. It has been a lot dealing with visas, packing and a new landlord overseas, so apologies for the lack of communication over the past few weeks. I also had to take Robert to Baltimore which was very bittersweet. Remember when I got him for you? You loved him so much, even though he was such a bitch. Ha.

Tomorrow, I am no longer a New Yorker. I know when we moved to California and how excited we were for a fresh start we said that and when I looked in the mirror and said it to myself again this morning, it made me think of you.

Remember when we moved to California? It's all I can think about as I pack my life up once again and head out into the great unknown. We were so excited. After working our asses off for so long in the big city and not feeling fulfilled, we decided that we were going to parts unknown – you transferred your high profile fashion job to your Los Angeles offices and I was determined to be the next big television writer. We were so hopeful then. We left New York in January, when it was so cold, and knew that when we got to sunny California our dreams would come true. Do you remember how much fun we had on the way out there? Stopping so many times to take pictures with the most random and ridiculous things. I found a few pictures that I thought I had deleted when I was looking through my phone the other day. I had traveled across the country twice already promoting my books but you never had and the look on your face and reaction to "seeing America" is something that I will never forget. We were so optimistic about our future, but when we got to California and reality set in and life happened it was far too much for us to handle together. I certainly hope that this new experience does not result more of the same. I am, for the first time since we moved to California, hopeful again. Hopeful that I am not only making the right decision, but that my future will be brighter across the pond. Maybe moving to California was really the big break I needed, just not in the way I thought I needed it.

I can't help but think of you during this time. It's so funny to me how life has worked out for me. When you left me, I was in the depths of despair. I thought that I would never move on, that I would never find my place in this world again because our lives were so entangled in each other and I thought I would never be able to love myself again. I've done all of those things and more. I'm still not over you and I'm not certain that I ever will be. But, perhaps this move will bring on a finality for me. Living in New York but not being together, I always lingered around the places that we used to go to together in hopes that we would "accidentally" bump into each other. I'd stalk your Instagram. Every time my phone would buzz, I would hope it would be you. It's so weird because I remember telling Sandra about what happened between the two of us and how you handled things and she said to me: "anyone else would hate Gretchen for what she's done and yet, you still love and forgive her". I told her it was because I truly loved you unconditionally. She did not care for that. Moving to London, I won't have those things anymore. I won't have an American telephone, nothing there will make me think of you because we have never been there together before and I won't walk down the street in hopes of bumping into you. This is good for me, as you are getting married and it truly is past time for me to move forward with my life.

You probably won't hear from me for a bit because I will be doing my best to get settled and starting a new job. I love you so much Gretchen, I still do, more and more every day. I can't explain why. I know you have moved on, but I seriously hope that you can get over the resentments that you have toward me. Not for me, but for yourself. You will never be able to fully give yourself to Larry or any other person if you hang on to what was or what could have been. The past is in the past and while I will never stop loving or caring for you, I have let go of the ill will I feel toward you and I hope that you can do the same for me.

I sent you a copy of my latest book (it comes out in two months – holy shit!). I hope you enjoy reading it as much as I enjoyed writing it.

I love you Gretchen

Twitter:

August 31, 2015

@maxrobertsauthor: Without darkness, there will never be light. Off to start my new life in London. Peace.

From: Gretchen Edwards
To: Max Roberts
RE: This Made Me Think of You
September 02, 2015 at 3:49 PM

Max –

I got the copy of your manuscript in the mail. When I opened it, I was as excited as a kid on Christmas morning. It was so nicely bound and fancy. It made me think of the time we got the first printed copy of your book in the mail and how we celebrated that amazing milestone. What an awesome night that was.

However, when I opened the book, I was surprised at what I found inside. Two hundred and seventy-five pages that just said *"I love you Gretchen"* over and over again. I had to hide it from Larry. What were you thinking? Did you even write a book? Are you even in London right now? I am not entirely sure I believe much of anything that is going on.

If you've arrived safely in London and can shoot me an email to explain, I would really appreciate it.

Gretchen

From: Gretchen Edwards
To: Max Roberts
RE: This Made Me Think of You
September 04, 2015 at 6:09 PM

Max –

I hope you're OK. I haven't heard from you since you left. I know you said you were going to be off the grid getting your life together, but we really need to speak.

I phoned the publishing house in London that you said you would be working for and they confirmed that you were starting next week. So at least I know you aren't lying about that. As far as the book is concerned, is this real? Or do you just not want me to read the real thing? I don't know why you wouldn't, as I have always been there to help in the past and even though we aren't together anymore, would still certainly love to be of service. You know how much I love your work.

Please let me know what's going on,

Gretchen

From: Gretchen Edwards
To: Max Roberts
RE: This Made Me Think of You
September 14, 2015 at 8:59 PM

Max –

Something happened the other day and I feel the need to tell you what's going. Claire and I went to try on wedding dresses and I had a complete and total breakdown.

I put on this lovely dress that suited me very nicely. When I turned around to view myself in the mirror, I completely lost it. I broke down in tears and Claire literally had to talk me off of a ledge. I told her that I couldn't marry Larry. He wasn't you. It wasn't the right thing to do. We went out for coffee afterwards and I unloaded everything on her and I feel the need to tell you everything that I said to her. I don't know what the fuck my problem is and why it took trying on wedding dresses to make me to realize this.

We walked down the street, myself in hysterics, Claire wondering where this lunatic standing next to her had suddenly come from, and I told her that I had made a huge mistake. She had to physically hold me up as we walked down the street. No one, outside of you, has ever seen me like that. I felt like I had somehow reverted back to freshman year of college and I was the meek, shy, young girl who could not deal with her problems. You helped me get rid of that girl years ago and now she came roaring back in full force. We sat and I finally calmed down and was able to tell her what was going on.

I had never told Claire that I had had an abortion in California. She's just not that kind of friend, I guess. I guess none of my friends are those kinds of friends because the only kind of friend I've ever had like that was you. So when I told her, she was completely shocked. "How could you do that?" she asked me. I told her that we were being horrible to each other out there and I did not think that bringing a child into this world at that time was the right thing to do. She told me that it was inexcusable to not tell you beforehand and, for whatever reason, her saying that really struck a chord with me. She was right. In fact, you were right. I was completely wrong. Maybe I was so disgusted with my decision that I felt the need to put all of this on you. You were going through a hard time and being mean. People go through hard times and you're right in saying that we hurt the people we love the most, because look at what I've done to you. I used your anger as an exit strategy because I was so ashamed of what I had done.

To make matters worse, I told her that I had basically strung you along for the past year. Telling you that I needed time, offering to help you and never doing so, and pretty much being a complete bitch. No matter what happened, you never overreacted after we broke up. You were fighting for me and I was fighting back for no reason whatsoever.

When we broke up, I did everything you're "supposed to do after a breakup". I went out, I made new friends, I buried myself in work and with that began traveling all of the time. I did what everyone around told me I needed to do, but the people around me weren't you. You were there, patiently waiting, and I stupidly pushed you away for no reason other than the fact that I had made a decision and was relentless in the fact that I was sticking to it. I made a choice that you had no control over and it seemed to ruin your life. I can't imagine how that must have felt. I made new friends and gallivanted around town like I was a twenty-one year old who had just broken up with a guy she had been sleeping with for a few months, not a thirty-one year old woman who had crushed the only person who had truly ever been there for her. You were my life and I was yours and I ripped that away from us. I don't know if I was trying to be staunch with my stubbornness or if I was just pissed about California, but it's all in the past. You are my future – not my past.

This was what I was thinking when Claire dropped me off at my apartment. When I got in, I sat on my bed and thought to myself: *No, I am overacting. Women have reservations about getting married when they try on dresses and everything ends up just fine.* I had a horrible headache so I laid down in bed and reached into my nightstand drawer to see if I had any pain reliever available. I stuck my hand in there and searched around but found none. In the back of the nightstand, I found a postcard that said: *Greetings from Atlantic City* on the front and on the back said: *This Made Me Think of You — M.* I'd never seen it before. Larry must have gotten it in the mail and never showed me. It was a sign.

I am going to break things off with Larry tonight after he gets home. I am not completely sure how he is going to take things, but I have to. I do not love him. I never have. I love you and always have. I thought that my being mad at you was going to be the be-all-end-all and it's just not so. This isn't right.

I've made a huge mistake.

Gretchen

Facebook:

September 15, 2015 at 3:17 PM

Gretchen Edwards is now single.

From: Gretchen Edwards
To: Max Roberts
RE: This Made Me Think of You
September 22, 2015 at 7:15 PM

Max —

Every time I call your office your secretary says you're out and you never respond to my messages. Are you not getting these emails?

I broke things off with Larry. He did not take things well. I told him right after I sent my last message to you. The following day, I moved out. Claire said I couldn't stay with her and Bruce because Bruce was pissed that I had done this to Larry. I am really never in town so I put my things back in storage and have just decided to stay in cheap hotels on the weekends until I figure something permanent out.

This weekend I did not stay in New York, however. When I got back from my latest and most exotic trip to Detroit, I got off the plane, took the subway to Port Authority and got on the bus to Atlantic City, just like we used to do. The entire ride down, the only thing I thought about was you. Remember how every time we went to Atlantic City, you used to regale me with stories of "the good old days of Atlantic City" as if you were either alive during them or you were some sort of Atlantic City aficionado? You'd tell me stories of all of the mobsters who used to line The Boardwalk, what now torn down hotel used to be where and the story of the invention of salt water taffy. God, I miss your stupid anecdotes.

Once I got there, I used the free money they give you on the bus to gamble (and lost) and then I wandered The Boardwalk as if I were looking for you. I know London is nice and all but AC is so far, how are you ever going to get back to you favorite place? By boat? I walked for hours, looking at all of the tacky shops that line the boards, looking at all of

Atlantic City's finest and just thought of all of the fun that we used to have together there. That really was our spot. Remember that time we got our palms read and the alleged psychic told me that someone with the initials "M.R." was going to betray me? Little did we know that it would be quite the opposite.

No one ever really understood why we liked it there so much, but it was like this unspoken thing that only you and I had. No one else ever got it. Sandra never got it. Larry most certainly would never get it. I slept in my hotel room that looked out onto the ocean alone that night. Every time I rolled over, I imagined you there.

I haven't stopped thinking about you since I broke up with you. I know that that sounds stupid considering the way that I have handled things in the past year, but it's true. Sleeping there alone, all I could think about was how you said you were going to propose to me there and I cried myself to sleep. I really did think about that all of the time. I know that I practically ignored you when you told me that you were going to propose to me, but I swear to God, I thought about it all of the time. The timing just wasn't right and I was being incredibly stubborn.

I am so stupid for doing this. I gave up the life I had with the most wonderful man I have ever met in the world because of a few stupid fights and nasty exchanges. There will never be anyone else like you. I fucked up.

Please respond to me

Gretchen

From: Gretchen Edwards
To: Max Roberts
RE: This Made Me Think of You
September 29, 2015 at 3:34 PM

Max –

I haven't heard from you since you left. Please return my calls or at the very least respond to one of my emails. I am pouring my heart out here and I'm getting nothing in return. I know, I know, you did for so long and I took it for granted, but I need to work this out with you.

None of my friends will talk to me because of this. Claire is being a complete bitch about this and has turned Becky against me too. I feel like I have no one here. To make matters worse, I am currently writing this email to you from a shit hotel room on Canal Street and I am pretty sure that someone was murdered in this room either last night or right before I checked in. I don't know why I listened to those bitches anyway. When we broke up they were like, "go out, have fun, meet someone". Why would someone whose never dated anyone but the same person for the past ten years need to do that? It's probably the reason why I jumped into my relationship with Larry so quickly – I didn't know any better. Not that that's an excuse, but I fucked up. Please!

I guess this is what I get for not listening to you in the first place. I told you I wanted to take a break and a year later, it is the biggest regret I have ever had. I don't know what I was thinking – jumping into this relationship with Larry, running around town, ignoring you. I was so incredibly selfish and wish I had just taken a moment to listen to what you were saying. You said everything that I ever wanted to hear and I don't know why I had such a hard time processing it. For Christ's sake, you gave me a cat that I have barely acknowledged existed in the past year and will now probably never be able to see again. I thought seeing Robert would trigger unhappy memories, but I know now that all it would have done would make me realize that I made a mistake and if I had seen him, it possibly would have sped the process of me realizing what an idiot I've been up. This behavior was not me.

Max – please respond to this. I really want to see you. I am thinking of even flying out to London to track you down. I know we haven't seen each other or even spoken over the phone in the past year, but I know this in my heart to be true: you are the only one for me. I know you think I gave up on you, but I promise you, I didn't!

I love you,

Gretchen

From: Gretchen Edwards
To: Max Roberts
RE: This Made Me Think of You
October 04, 2015 at 5:55 PM

Max –

I heard an Elvis song at the old diner that we used to go to today and this made me think of you. Remember when you used to sing that one song of his that I had never heard of until you sang it to me? It went: *when the evening shadows fall. And you're wondering who to call. For a little company. There's always me.* God, you used to sing that all the time and I had never heard it, unless you were singing it, until today. I don't even like Elvis for Christ's sake.

I'm sorry Max. I truly am. I fucked up and I should have listened to what you were saying all along. I was so selfish and wrong and you still by stood me, no matter what.

I booked a one-way flight to London for this weekend. I have no idea where you live, but I am going to find you.

All the love in the world,

Gretchen

From: Max Roberts
To: Gretchen Edwards
Greetings from London
October 05, 2015 at 4:45 AM

Gretchen –

I don't know if you and Larry have had a million children and moved to Connecticut yet, so I hope you are still at this address. I just wanted to let you know that I've settled into my new job and am really enjoying London.

I'm sorry I haven't returned any of your calls and I'm not sure if you've tried to email me or not but I've closed my old email account. Too many memories. Before my flight left to go to London, I checked my sent mail from the past few months and there were so many emails to you with the subject: "this made me think of you". I had to get rid of it in order to really have a fresh start. There was too much baggage for me in New York and I had to get out of there. Knowing that you were moving on with another man and that I was just a subway ride away to stop you was too much for me to bear. It wasn't healthy for me and so I have taken this move abroad as a fresh start. I'm making friends here and I love my job. It's truly wonderful.

Of course I miss you terribly and think of you every day still. I wish that afternoon last September had a different outcome and we had just had a lover's quarrel and moved on. If you had told me a year ago that I would be where I am now and without you, I would have never believed you. I fought so hard for you – harder than anything I had ever fought for before and I lost. I couldn't take the rejection any longer. There really is only so much a man can go through before he finally throws his hands in the air and yells "MERCY". I never thought I would give up on you – and I guess I will always hold out hope – but I simply couldn't put myself in that position any longer.

I'm sure you got the book I sent you. Clearly, it's not what will be published, but I wanted to pull one last practical joke on you and let you know how much I love you still.

I thought that moving to London would help relieve my feelings toward you but they haven't. Instead of walking the streets of New York thinking I may bump into you, I now walk the streets of London looking at places that we could be spending time together. I don't understand what's wrong with me. My love for you will never die. I guess it's just something that I will have to live with forever, even though we are practically a world apart.

I do still love you Gretchen and I promise you, I will call you very soon. I'm going to continue to get settled and I will buzz you in a few weeks.

Love you,

Max

Facebook:

October 11, 2015 at 12:27 PM

Gretchen checks in at London-Heathrow Airport

Facebook:

October 24, 2015 at 4:09 PM

Gretchen Edwards and Max Roberts are in a relationship.

From: Gretchen Edwards
To: Max Roberts
RE: This Made Me Think of You
December 31, 2015 at 1:12 PM

Max –

My love. You are sitting right next to me as I send this email and I couldn't be happier about it. In the last two months that we have lived together in London, it's like nothing that happened in the past has ever mattered and we have finally been able to get that fresh start that we both so desperately needed. Maybe we did need that time to work through our issues separately because as I peek over my laptop and look at you trying to take down the Christmas lights, I know that I have never loved you more than I do right this minute.

How wonderful that I was able to transfer my job to my company's London headquarters and that we have been able to cohabitate in a new country and experience all of these incredible new things together. I honestly cannot believe that you took me back, after everything that happened between us, but I am so grateful for it. I always say that I have no regrets in life and as far as the past year plus is concerned, I can honestly say I don't regret a thing. Yes, I acted completely out of character and so did you. But, had we not taken that break and gone through the experiences we had we would have never been able to find our way back to each other and have a bond that is now stronger than ever. All of the hurt and all of the pain was simply just a blessing in disguise because now I've never been happier and I know you feel the same. We are meant to be together and I am sorry that it took me being engaged to another man and you moving across the Atlantic Ocean to realize that.

Last year, when you started writing me emails of things that made you think of me, I acted as if I was annoyed by your correspondence, when in reality I very much looked forward to them. Remembering all of our fun times together always brought a tear to my eye. I know I said differently, but that was because I was confused about how I was feeling. No one has ever gone out of their way for me the way you have and I believe that no one ever will.

You truly are the love of my life. I will love you forever. You have made me the happiest woman in the world and I will never again second guess that. Thank you for being mine. I love you unconditionally. It's you and me against the world. Now and forever.

Forever,

Gretchen

P.S. Can't wait for our spring trip to AC. I'm putting all of my money on black! Xo

ACKNOWLEDGEMENTS

Michael Lazar, thank you for your beautiful cover design. You are a truly amazing artist and friend. Special thanks to Kathryn Owens, Katie Taddeucci, Amanda Patten and Irene Kheradi for your wisdom and support.

Big hugs and thanks to Tom and Michael D'Angora (as always), Eric Saggese, Evelyn Zilberman, Jennifer Tucker, Candace Gregory, Erik George, Shawn McCulloch, Ron de Jesus, Brendan McCann, Sally Schwab and Valerie Issembert. Thanks to my peeps in 652 for keeping me sane – Danielle Mumpower, Steve Jones, Ryan Howard and Hannah Dishman, xo!

Special thanks to my amazing parents Keith Rosenberg and Patricia Rafferty for your continuous love and support through the years. You have helped me so much, particularly in the past few months and I do not know what I would do without you. I'd dedicate this book to you both, if you hadn't had such amazing break-up stories yourself. I believe that warrants its own book, or series of books, rather. Shout outs to Carol and Billy for putting up with the both of you.

Thanks to my wonderful brothers, sisters, niece and nephews who I love more than anything: Tony, Nikki, Kim, Jamie, Kevin, Devon, Finn, Reed, Jolie and Blake. There are so fucking many of you.

Finally, thank you George Ewald. None of this would have ever happened without you. Literally

Made in the USA
Middletown, DE
02 May 2016